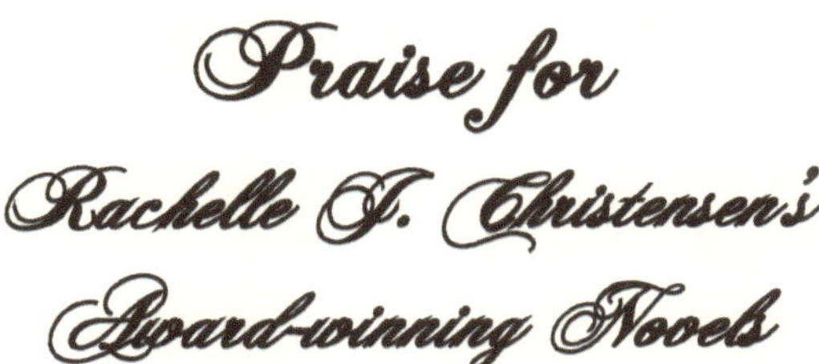

Praise for
Rachelle J. Christensen's
Award-winning Novels

Hawaiian Masquerade is the perfect summer read. Set on the beautiful island of Kauai, you will fall in love with the characters, the story line, the setting, and most of all the romance. I would highly recommend this fast-paced, fabulous clean romance.

--Cami Checketts, author of *The Feisty One: A Billionaire Bride Pact Romance*

Christensen has done a magnificent job of putting together an unlikely match and letting it challenge the characters to grow, change, and become better together than they were apart. This is a wonderful, sweet romance that you'll want to stay up to finish.

-Lucy McConnell, author of the *Billionaire Marriage Brokers* series

"SILVER CASCADE SECRETS is an exciting romantic suspense novella … Great writing, a sweet romance, and an intriguing mystery all rolled into a single story."

—Heather B. Moore *USA Today* Bestselling Author of *Finding Sheba*

"Just in time for fall, … romantic suspense which will tingle the spine and thrill the heart."
—DESERET NEWS, Melissa Demoux

"...A great read for a lazy Sunday afternoon. I highly recommend."
—Diane Darcy, USA Today bestselling author

"Don't expect to get a lot of sleep…If the thrills of the chase don't get you, the thrills of the heart will."
—J. Scott Savage, author of the Mysteries of Cove Series

"*Diamond Rings are Deadly Things* pulled me right in from the first page and held me captive until the very end. Great characters, a compelling plot, a surprising twist at the end... Rachelle Christensen knows how to craft a great mystery."
—*Tristi Pinkston, author of the Secret Sisters Mysteries*

Hawaiian
Masquerade
BURKE BILLIONAIRE ROMANCE

Hawaiian
BURKE BILLIONAIRE ROMANCE
Masquerade

Other Works by Rachelle

Diamond Rings Are Deadly Things (Wedding Planner Mysteries #1)

Veils and Vengeance (#2)

Proposals and Poison (#3)

The Soldier's Bride (A Music Box Romance #1)

Carve Me a Melody (A Music Box Romance #2)

Hawaiian Masquerade (Burke Billionaire Romance)

How to Fetch a Fiancé (Destination Billionaire Romance)

River Whispers

Wrong Number

Caller ID

Novellas:

Silver Cascade Secrets

Double Take

Hope for Christmas: An Echo Ridge Romance

The Kiss Thief: An Echo Ridge Romance

The Princess Bride of Riodan: An Echo Ridge Romance

Coming Home to Love: An Echo Ridge Romance

Hawaiian Masquerade

Rachelle J. Christensen

Hawaiian Masquerade

Original Cover Design: Steven Novak
Cover Design © Peachwood Press
Edited by: Jenna Roundy
Interior Book Design: Bob Houston eBook Formatting

ISBN-13: 978-0996897-65-5

Published by Peachwood Press, November 2017

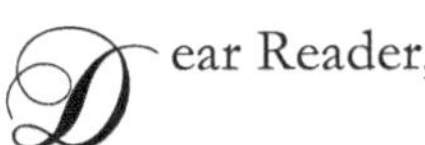

Introduction

$\mathcal{D}$ear Reader,

Hawaii is one of my favorite places to visit. The beach, the sunset, the amazing food, and the atmosphere make for a perfect combination to escape from reality. Add in a new book to read, and I'm truly in paradise.

It's not always possible to jet off to an exotic location filled with adventure and romance, but we can become immersed in a story that takes us to places we've never been. Every sentence transports us to another world. And the characters take residence in our heart while we travel with them on their journey.

In *Hawaiian Masquerade* you'll meet Lexi, a successful businesswoman who needs a change from the hectic pace of corporate life. And Derek, a handsome, local photographer who has an eye for beauty—but a chip on his shoulder when it comes to the wealthy. Embark with them on their journey to discover what—and who—they really want in life.

Please enjoy your adventure with Lexi and Derek in *Hawaiian Masquerade*.

Best wishes,
Kaylee Baldwin, author of *Hearts in Peril*

Foreword

I'm thrilled to write this foreword for Rachelle Christensen! I love her writing and the way she makes the characters feel real and makes you want to root for them!

I spoke with Rachelle about her writing process, because I always love to learn more about what makes other writers tick, and this is what she said, "Most of my novels are written in 25 minute sprints, one at a time. Creating is such a part of life for all of us, and I'm thankful that I'm able to share these stories that sometimes keep me up at night, infiltrate my dreams, and keep pushing me to the outer edges of creativity. *Hawaiian Masquerade* was particularly fun to write because my family helped me brainstorm the plot. My husband and I visited Kauai a few years ago, and the island is so alive! When I thought about setting this story in an exotic location, I knew it would be set in Kauai, because I can't wait to go back someday and visit again."

It's fun to see the fabric of life authors weave into each story. If you love the ocean, romance, and hot, hardworking men—you're going to love *Hawaiian Masquerade.*

Taylor Hart, author of *The Bachelor Billionaire Romances*

Dedication:

For Steve, because you inspire all my love stories.

Chapter 1

exi stared at the tube of cadmium red oil paint hanging from the shelf, remembering how expensive that color had seemed in college. She grabbed it and ten additional tubes in a rainbow of colors—the first step on a new path in life. The squeaking wheel of the shopping cart gave voice to the trepidation crawling up her spine, telling her she was nuts for leaving behind a life that most people claimed they wanted. But Lexi knew something that most people didn't: millions and millions of dollars did not create a wellspring of happiness. Cold hard cash was, in fact, cold and hard.

Kauai was not cold. The brilliant sunshine and perfumed air was freely available to everyone on the island. Roadways were drenched in color from vibrant greens to bright pinks and accented with the red dirt Kauai was known for. Lexi studied the brushes available and chose a long-handled round brush that would help her recreate the beautiful landscapes of the island. Now if she could find a few canvases, she would be ready to paint on the beach outside her home. She turned down another aisle and saw a display of white rectangles and squares. They were wrapped in plastic, but Lexi ran her finger along the edges; the rough feel of a blank canvas and the possibility it represented brought back pleasant memories.

A toddler's shrill cry snapped her out of her musings. She steered her cart around a stack of twelve-by-eighteen-inch canvases and found the source. The little girl couldn't have been more than two years old, tiny with fine black hair pulled back in pigtails. Her red hibiscus-print dress set off dark caramel skin, and even as her wail intensified, Lexi found herself admiring the pretty Polynesian girl.

That's when she noticed that the toddler was alone. Lexi glanced around, but this area of the store was empty. She stepped forward carefully and crouched in front of the girl. "Sweetie, are you lost?"

As soon as the words left her mouth, the little girl held out her arms and reached for Lexi. She sniffled, melting Lexi's heart as she carefully picked up the child. She looked down the aisle, hoping to see the little girl's mother, but at the same time nervous that the mother would think her daughter was being kidnapped. Lexi patted the girl's back, and she snuggled closer. Swallowing against the sudden lump in her throat, Lexi focused on the task at hand.

Turning slowly to scan the store again, she saw a man with dark hair, a chiseled jawline, and a worried crease in his forehead. He was tall with golden-brown skin and wore a green tank top that showed off his finely sculpted biceps. Something shifted in Lexi's heart. It thumped hard twice, and blood rose to her cheeks. The man stared back at her, his face open, revealing an arc of emotions as he took in the sight of the little girl and Lexi—wonder, admiration, curiosity, and something else she couldn't define.

She stepped forward, eyebrows raised in question. "Is she yours?"

His dark hair was spiked on top and close-shaven on the sides. He sported a bit of scruff that Lexi could only describe as sexy. One side of his mouth lifted, and he shook his head. "No, is she lost?"

"Yes, she was crying right over here, and I've stayed put for a minute hoping her mom would show up looking for her."

He turned around in a slow circle, repeating the search Lexi had undertaken moments before, having a better view over the shelves because he was taller. Oh, so tall and sculpted. "I can help you find her parents. This store isn't that big. Maybe they haven't missed her yet."

Lexi's brow furrowed in protest as she struggled to rein in her emotions. It had been at least three minutes since she'd heard the toddler's cries, and five minutes was like an eternity in a child's world—surely it would feel just as long for a frantic parent searching for her child. She gently patted the girl's back. "It's okay, sweetie, I know what it feels like to be lost," she murmured. Then she realized that the man was standing close enough to hear her. She straightened, cleared her throat, and spoke louder. "We'll help you."

The man pointed to the other side of the store. "I'll go this way, you go that way?"

"That's a good idea." Lexi smiled, and her stomach flipped when the man returned her smile. The little girl moved her head, quiet and warm in Lexi's arms.

The man walked quickly across the store, and Lexi went in the other direction. There was only one other shopper, an old man with a handful of charcoal and sketch pads. Lexi smiled at him, and he winked at her and the little girl. "Beautiful kaikamahine."

Lexi nodded, appreciating the melodic Hawaiian language. The man saw them as mother and daughter, which was a stretch considering Lexi's fair skin, blond hair, and green eyes. She held the child close. They were two lost souls trying to find something to keep them safe. Lexi was certain she'd find the little girl's mother, but what could Lexi find that would fill the need in her heart?

"Here she is," someone said from behind Lexi. She turned around and saw that the dark-haired man was leading a Polynesian woman with long dark hair toward her. "Safe and sound."

"Keilani! Oh, baby," the woman said. "I'm so glad you're okay."

The little girl immediately sat up and reached her arms out. She cried for a few seconds, clinging to her mother, clutching her light cotton shirt.

"Mahalo. Oh, thank you so much for finding my baby," the woman gushed.

"She's a sweetheart," Lexi said. "She wanted me to hold her, and that seemed to help while we looked for you."

"One minute she was there, and then she was gone. You know how kids are." The woman patted her daughter's back. "Keilani, say thank you to the beautiful lady who found you," the woman said, looking down at her daughter with a smile.

The toddler looked at Lexi and held her hand out, moving it back and forth. Then she giggled and blew Lexi a kiss.

Lexi pretended to catch the kiss in the air and patted her cheek. "Thank you, Keilani. Have fun shopping."

She waved at the little girl, then let her hand drop to her side. That's when she noticed the man who had helped her standing quietly next to the end cap of paintbrushes on aisle seven. "You really get the credit for finding her," Lexi said. "Thanks for hunting down the lost mother."

He grinned. "Glad to help out a tourist when I can."

"But I'm not a tourist," Lexi replied. "I just moved here."

One eyebrow lifted, and Lexi noticed a shift in his brown eyes, as if he were seeing her for the first time. He held out his hand. "That's great news. Aloha, and welcome to Kauai. I'm Derek Mitchell."

They shook hands, and a sensation like warm, salty spray went up her arm. When they broke contact, she immediately craved his touch again. What was happening to her? The first hot guy to shake her hand had her thinking of moonlight walks on the beach and kisses in the sand. She decided that she was smitten with the *idea* of this Hawaiian guy. She needed a can of chocolate-covered macadamia nuts and a long bath, not a man. Still, she smiled broadly and returned the introduction. "I'm Lexi Burke, no longer from Chicago."

Derek wrinkled his nose. "Man, that place is cold. Good choice coming here in March. The weather will only get better from now until October."

"I'm counting on it," Lexi replied.

"Are you an artist?" Derek asked, motioning to the growing stack of supplies in Lexi's cart, which she'd left in the middle of the aisle.

"I wish." Lexi laughed as she grabbed the handle. "Maybe in a different lifetime—or maybe now. I love art, and I need to refocus some of my energy. Drawing and painting used to be a passion of mine, before the nine-to-five killed it."

Derek nodded. "I get that. The good thing about this place is it unwinds all that tension, and creativity leaks out from everywhere." He tipped his head to the side. "Since you're new, I'll let you in on a secret. Drive over to Hanapepe tomorrow—Friday night is the local art night—and you'll see what I mean."

"Hmm, I may just do that." Lexi gave Derek her canned response to every invite from the male species. And then she realized that he was being friendly. Maybe she could go . . . but then she might run into him, and he was too good-looking with that bronzed skin and his relaxed stance that seemed to say, *I don't have any idea what my looks do to your pulse rate.* Yep. Derek was on her list of things not to encounter in Kauai. Her fingertips drummed along the plastic-wrapped handle of her shopping cart, trying to keep up with her racing heart. It was time to make a quick exit. "Thanks again for your help. Maybe I'll see you around the island sometime."

"Good luck with the painting." Derek lifted one hand and let it fall. He had a stack of frames tucked under his other arm.

After checking out and packing the supplies into her Jeep, Lexie wished she hadn't been so skittish around Derek and missed the opportunity to reciprocate his interest in her new hobby. He'd spoken about creativity, and judging by the frames and his knowledge of the Hanapepe street fair, he was probably an artist himself. There she was, thinking about him again. Derek was just another piece of man candy Lexi didn't want to taste, even if he'd been kind and genuine at the store. She shouldn't be mean to him just because she carried a chip on her shoulder the size of the Sears Tower. She could give him the benefit of the doubt. Derek was quite possibly delicious on the inside, too.

Then again, so was the authentic Hawaiian shaved ice Lexi was going to pick up at Hee Fat General Store. Yes, ice covered in sugar sitting on top of a mountain of thick ice cream would definitely do the trick to keep Lexi's mind from wandering into dangerous territory.

Chapter 2

That moment when Derek had walked out of the end of the aisle and saw Lexi had stayed with him all day. He remembered how her straight blond hair fell across her shoulders when she crouched down and asked the child if she needed help. The way the little girl had put her arms around Lexi's neck made Derek wish for his camera. Lexi had hesitated only a second before embracing the tiny girl, gently holding her as she stood and surveyed the store. That was the first time she'd seen him, and her striking jade-colored eyes had lit up with hope.

That Lexi thought the little girl could be his touched him in a way he'd never admit. His last relationship had ended when Carly claimed he was too self-absorbed and obsessed with photography to ever be a decent father. The accusation stung because, when the time came, nothing in the world would be more important than being a father. If Carly had been the right woman, she would have seen that in him.

His thoughts strayed to Lexi and the likelihood of seeing her again. The odds were slim, despite his desire to photograph her stunning face. The light and shadow of sunset across her delicate bone structure were as easy to imagine as listening to the musical quality of her sweet voice that soothed children and awakened his bruised heart.

Derek ran his fingers over the coarse sides of his hair. He needed to focus on preparations for art night in Hanapepe. Why had he blurted out an invitation to Lexi for art night? He'd probably spend the better part of the evening looking for her golden hair. Derek groaned. *Focus, dude!* He'd been studying ideas on how to make a bigger splash at the street festival. Last week hadn't gone well, making him question continuing. But he'd invested so much in his booth and producing the photos to sell. He decided he'd give it two more weeks and see if he could break even on the venture.

It was more than just an art fair to Derek. He wanted to make things work in Kauai. He'd lived here for two years now, scraping by, working odd jobs to pay the electric bill and keep from going hungry and photographing on the side.

Even though he was only a quarter Hawaiian, Kauai was in his blood. His grandfather—or kupuna—was born on this island and buried in the Kauai Veterans Cemetery on Lele Road. Derek had visited Kauai once when he was in his teens and indulging in a rebellious streak. His parents had sent him to the island to be straightened out by his kupuna's old-fashioned ways. Derek's life had been different since then, and in a way, he'd spent the rest of his life trying to make it back to the island full of beautiful secrets. Derek knew he could work the rest of his life and barely scratch the surface of the possibilities for his photography business. It brought him a joy that was hard to explain. Now if only someone else would find joy in his work so that he could afford to continue his dream.

Derek straightened the folding table set up in his living room, scattered with photography supplies. He dusted off the set of picture frames housing some of his best pieces with a worn and torn T-shirt. Tonight he would find an opportunity that would change things. Derek wasn't ready to give up on his dream to shoot photos full-time. His kupuna expected more of him than that.

"Why so many thoughts, bro?" Pika asked as he barged through the front door of Grandpa's old house. Pika was full-blooded Hawaiian and perfect for a postcard with his six-foot-two height, bulging arms, and wavy black hair.

Derek rubbed his face and grunted. His friend and roommate was laid-back, but he always knew when something was eating at Derek. "Just thinking I don't want to be chopping bamboo with a machete next week, ya know?"

Pika shook his head. "Money's money, right?"

"I'd rather be shooting, catching the light in the lens." Derek held up his thumb and index finger. "I feel like I'm this close. If I could just catch a break . . ."

"Now that's what we need to do. Surf," Pika said. "That's the only way I know to catch a break."

Derek rolled his eyes. Pika was the epitome of Hawaiian culture. He was at peace with himself and life on the island. It was a gift that Derek wished he could indulge in, but they were wired differently. Derek wanted to climb the mountain and conquer the world, and Pika was content to work the same job he'd worked as a teenager, chopping coconuts in the shade at the base of that mountain. Pika's way made good money, selling the coconuts to the tourists hiking the coastline. Through his consistent hard labor he was making more money than Derek, and he seemed happy, too.

"Did you ask your mom about making some frames?" Derek asked.

Pika held up a canvas bag that he'd set near the door. "My makuahine, she get all excited and made you two already. I hope they fit." He pulled out two frames woven from palm leaves and set them in front of Derek.

Derek picked one up and ran his finger along the intricate braiding; the texture was unique, and the color was a dark green. They would fit the eight-by-ten photos printed on foamcore he'd ordered last week. "This is perfect. I really think this will work." He stood and slapped Pika on the back. "Thanks, man."

Pika flashed him the hang-ten sign. "She's still weaving, so if they don't sell, I don't want to know."

Derek grinned. "Tell her to make ten more."

When the door swung shut behind Pika, Derek got to work fitting his photographs carefully into the hand-woven frames. Everyone wanted a souvenir from their travels, but most tourists were tired of the cheap, generic merchandise that was all made in China. People wanted a piece of the island to take home with them. Something created in Kauai. A unique piece that carried a sense of sinking your toes into the warm, white sand. Derek grabbed his camera and set up an impromptu shoot of his new line of products: custom frames holding custom pictures from the isle of Kauai.

When he leaned in to focus the lens, he thought of Lexi's cheek pressed against the girl's dark hair, her eyes full of worry and her lips cooing comfort, and he fumbled with his camera.

What was it about that shot he couldn't get out of his head? Shaking himself, Derek concentrated on capturing the perfect photo, but all the while thoughts of Lexi reflected off of every surface.

Chapter 3

The sound of ocean swells was interrupted by a rooster crowing right outside Lexi's window. She groaned and rolled over, peering at the warm light flooding through the screen on her balcony. Her eyes felt like they were full of the fine sand of the Kauai beach outside, and the thought made her smile. She was here. In Kauai. To stay.

Lexi sat up in bed. On the floor was a swarm of boxes that trailed into the hall of the three-bedroom home. There was a path that led to the door of the balcony overlooking the prime real estate territory on the shore of Princeville, Kauai. She had purchased the house and beachside property for four million dollars in her desire to escape from the cold and brutal winter of Chicago—and the cold and brutal reality that had become her life. Lexi shook her head. She wouldn't think of that right now.

Her body groaned against the shift in time zones, but Lexi rolled out of bed to get ready for the day. She brushed through her long hair, freshly highlighted with golden streaks in preparation for the Hawaiian sun. When she applied a smudge of green eyeshadow that accented the jade color of her eyes, she thought of Derek's brown eyes. A thrill fluttered through her stomach, and she smiled, remembering how he'd casually told her about art night in Hanapepe.

After Derek had mentioned it to her, she'd done some homework and found that the open-air art gallery, also known as a street fair, was held every Friday in the laid-back style of the Hawaiian culture. Come, eat, enjoy, and be. That's exactly what Lexi wanted to do, so she'd made up her mind to attend. She wasn't going to look for Derek among the artists showcasing their wares. No, she was going because she wanted to experience life on Kauai and maybe meet a few local artists. It'd be fun to find someone who offered painting classes or join a group to help her remember the skills she'd learned so long ago.

After rummaging through a bag for her favorite tie-dyed headband, Lexi stood still, unsure of what to do with the hours unplanned and yawning before her. Even though her home was in disarray—boxes seemed to multiply like the chickens she'd seen foraging along the shoreline last night—Lexi was free. The peacefulness of her surroundings came from the absence of her cell phone buzzing constantly with texts, emails, appointment reminders, Skype chats, and desperate late-night phone calls from businesses trying to get their product imported from China before they ran out of inventory. Lexi's shoulders tightened at the thought, and she quickly crossed the room and stepped out onto the balcony, inhaling the soft, flower-scented air. Blowing out a breath and repeating the process, Lexi rinsed from her soul the reminders of her former life as a top executive in her brother's import and export company.

Jordan Burke Enterprises had risen quickly, and her brother had snatched her up fresh from college to fill in all the gaps of a growing business. But none of those things had filled the gaps in her own life, and now at age thirty-two, Lexi had escaped with enough money to lounge on the beach for the rest of her life. She took in another cleansing breath. The niggling doubt circling in her brain asked again and again if she was crazy, if she would last more than a week without the frantic pace of the office and some kind of mental stimulation. Over the past year, she'd often had trouble sleeping because her mind was whirring with so many ideas, but that part of her was drained. That's why she'd purchased the art supplies. The box of paints and brushes would feed her creative side, which had been starved into submission. Hopefully after a few months, she could find a healthy balance between a different kind of work and creating.

All she had right now was her brother; her best friend, Gracie; and hundreds of millions of dollars. Lexi straightened. She wouldn't be defined by her money, success, or business ties in Kauai. Today was the first day of the rest of her life, and she planned to make it memorable.

She headed to the kitchen for breakfast and heard an electronic alert sound. The interruption to her solitude was so foreign that Lexi actually checked the front door before realizing that the noise had come from her new cell phone sitting in the charging dock on the granite countertop. She brushed a finger over the screen to see an incoming text from Shawn Halstrom.

I know I said I wouldn't contact you, but I forgot that there's an extra key fob in a box

under the passenger seat of the Jeep. I didn't want you to lose it. I hope you find what you're looking for in paradise. Miss you. I never thought it would be this hard to let you go.

Lexi sighed. Her personal assistant, Shawn, had handled almost every detail of her move. Shawn wanted her to stay and be part of his life in a personal and romantic way. Even though Shawn was one of the few men she trusted wasn't after her money, he couldn't persuade her to stay. They'd circled around the idea of dating for months before Lexi finally gave in and went to dinner with him. That began a fledgling relationship challenged daily by their grueling workload.

Months after a stilted and pathetic breakup, Shawn maintained that they didn't get a chance to see if a relationship would work. That was probably true, but Shawn was eager to climb the Burke Enterprise ladder, vying for a position that would lead to the stressful job Lexi happily abandoned, and she didn't want to be a part of that—even vicariously—any longer.

The first three days away from the office, Lexi was like an addict going through withdrawal. No one needed her. It was strange, and on the fourth day Lexi realized it could be strangely wonderful.

She held her phone, her finger hovering over the screen. Should she reply or keep the distance she'd requested? She imagined Shawn in a designer suit, blond highlights in his dark hair, his chiseled jawline lifting in a commanding smile. She missed him, too—the familiarity of him. He'd worked overtime helping her plan everything, supporting the decision that she knew he didn't agree with, because he was a good guy. She almost texted him a silly joke for old time's sake, but she decided a simple thank-you would be courteous and keep the lines clear. She sent the text and put her phone back on the charging dock.

Her stomach grumbled, redirecting her focus onto food. Her fridge needed help—the bag of mangoes and stack of yogurt looked lonely on the pristine shelves. While Lexi ate, she jotted down a grocery list. In Chicago, her money had made it possible for her to work herself into overdrive. She never cooked, cleaned, or shopped, and she hired someone to take care of picking up the dry cleaning. Sitting in the middle of her spacious kitchen, Lexi asked herself again what she'd missed in life because of her money.

She spent a few hours unpacking in the solitude with the ocean breeze and crashing waves as her company. Two weeks ago, she'd spent Friday night working until one in the morning at Burke Enterprises, trying to play catch-up after Chinese New Year and the mandatory lapse in production for all factories in China. February was one of the most stressful months of the year. It was March, and she was already planning how she would celebrate the Chinese New Year next year.

Lexi lifted the flaps of another box and hesitated, smiling. The box was full of forgotten art supplies. When she was in college, she'd taken some classes and dabbled in graphic design, but then she'd been lured into the business management track by her brother. There just hadn't been time for anything as creative as oil painting or sketching since then.

Lexi spent a couple hours sorting through notebooks, sketch pads, and detailed instructions on mixing colors and practicing with her color wheel. She found an old textbook and a notebook full of detailed instructions from classes she'd attended. Reading through the notes made her fingers itch to paint. Lexi took it as a sign. It was time to follow her creative soul to a new vista.

She glanced at the clock. It was also time to get cleaned up. Lexi scrambled to shower and dress for the evening. Her stomach buzzed with anticipation. There was something waiting for her in Hanapepe tonight—she could almost taste it.

The drive from her new home in Princeville to the street fair seemed like a dream. Dark green foliage, bright purple flowers, and glorious archways as trees tangled together over the road. Yellow plumeria and bougainvillea in a shade of fuchsia that almost didn't seem real flashed by on her way to Hanapepe. By the time Lexi reached the tiny island city, the sunset streaking orange and pink across the sky, she felt like she was walking outside her skin. A smile that would have seemed out of place on Lexi last week kept tugging at the corners of her mouth.

She drove past a grassy area and parked next to several other vehicles. Even though Shawn had practically begged Lexi to stay, he'd done an excellent job of helping her relocate, even finding her a used vehicle in the area. The Jeep was perfect for blending in; Lexi especially loved the rust spots on the sides of the faded blue doors. She hopped down from the driver's seat and started across the tall grass toward the booths, meandering through the area. Lexi left her lingering feelings for Shawn behind and smoothed out her flowing skirt. Around three hundred people visited vendors' booths set up in front of the shops, eating, laughing, and dancing. Lexi flipped her blond braid over her shoulder. She was ready to step into this life.

Tiki torches and Hawaiian music provided an ambiance that loosened the knots in Lexi's shoulders. The smell of barbeque had her mouth watering. She stopped by a stand selling cups of fresh pineapple and mango. Lexi purchased one and savored the sweet tropical flavors of the island. Another store sold jewelry, and Lexi selected a bracelet with beads made from local wood, shell, and rocks. The woman slipped it on her wrist after she paid, and Lexi murmured, "Mahalo."

The woman nodded. "Mahalo to you, too, beautiful island girl."

The sentiment warmed Lexi, and she found herself smiling easily as she browsed. She passed a photography booth, another jewelry vendor, and one selling sun hats that she was tempted to purchase. Near the end of the street, she approached a stand for Fuse Photography. The logo was cool, featuring a camera sitting on top of a sea turtle with a fuse igniting the business title. She studied it for a moment longer, thinking of the many marketing meetings she'd attended to get the perfect logo on the right piece of merchandise made in China. It was nice to appreciate something that she didn't have to stress over.

"Aloha. If you like my sign, I bet you'll like the photos even more." A man stood behind a table of photographs, packaged and ready to sell—the photos, that is, although the man was pretty well put together, too, from what she could see. The torch was blocking her view. "It's Lexi, right?" He extended his hand. "Remember me, from the art store?"

Lexi stepped out from under the bright light, and Derek's face came into focus. Her breath caught at the sight of him, and she smiled, reaching out to him. "Yes. Derek—finder of lost parents. You didn't mention you had a booth here when you told me about art night."

Derek grinned and motioned to his T-shirt, the Fuse logo stretching nicely across his muscular build. "Now you know."

Lexi admired his casual stance. He seemed at home amid his photographs. "That is a great logo. So what kind of photography do you specialize in?"

Derek smiled and extended his arm, indicating the spread of pictures. "Mostly nature scenes, but I'd say I specialize in underwater photography." He tapped a close-up of a sea turtle.

Lexi stepped closer. "That is so cool. I've always wanted to swim with sea turtles." She traced her finger over the plastic wrapping.

"This guy was a little grumpy about having his picture taken, but it was a nice shot."

Lexi laughed at the seeming frown on the turtle's face. She set it down and picked up another photo of a group of turtles in the water, some reaching for the surface amidst a school of yellow-and-black fish. "I'd like to buy this one. It's such a unique shot."

Derek brightened. "Thanks. That one is twenty-eight dollars."

Lexi took out a twenty and a ten. "Keep the change. That's an excellent price for a photo of this caliber."

He took the twenty and pulled out two dollars in change. "It's the going rate on this island for photography. I'm glad you like it."

Lexi shook her head. "No, I'm serious. I stopped by a couple other booths and I can tell the difference."

Derek hesitated, the two dollars in his outstretched palm, and Lexi had the distinct impression that he worked hard for every dollar in his business. She'd been there once upon a time, but it'd been so long since she'd worried about the minutiae of daily life that two dollars seemed a paltry tip for the handsome photographer.

She decided to change the subject. Holding the photo under the lights strung up around his booth, she examined it again. "How do you take pictures underwater? Is it a waterproof camera?"

"Nah, much better." He grinned and carefully folded the two dollars, returning them to his cash box. "It's pretty awesome. I have this case that snaps around my camera, so I get the quality I want without having to spend thousands on a waterproof camera that can actually take decent shots."

"Really? That sounds pretty ingenious," Lexi said. She glanced to the side, not wanting to take up his time if there were other people waiting to look at the photographs, but this end of the street fair was quiet. "This is kind of embarrassing to admit, but I don't even know how to snorkel."

Derek laughed. "Well, that's one of the top activities for tourists around here."

"But remember, I'm not a tourist." Lexi put her hand to the side of her mouth. "I'm a local."

"You mentioned before you're from Chicago? Miss the weather yet?" He winked.

Lexi held out her bare arm, stark white against her pink tank top. "It may take me a while to look like a native, but it sure is nice to go outside without a coat on."

"There's a few places on this island you'll want a jacket," Derek said. "It rains every day at the Wai'ale'ale Crater."

"Hey, I read about that. The wettest place on earth."

"That's the one." He picked up another photo and held it out to her. "Here's a shot of the crater right after a rainstorm when the sun decided to peek out."

Lexi took the photo and gasped at the pure beauty before her. The guidebook she had read had a couple photos and descriptions, but they didn't come close to the depiction she held in her hand. Dozens of crystal-white waterfalls spouted from the mountain, made up of one dark green verdant ridge after another. A cloud hovered near the edges of the crater. Lexi could almost feel the moisture in the air. "This is breathtaking."

"A lot of the rich people with too much money to burn take helicopter rides over this crater, but you can't get a shot like this unless you're standing still."

Not missing the resentment in his description, Lexi asked, "So you hiked up to a vantage point for the shot?"

Derek nodded. "The hikes on this island are amazing."

The photograph was twelve by sixteen inches and marked at fifty-five dollars. She wanted to buy it for her front entryway, but Derek's comment about rich people made her hold back.

What would he think if he knew Lexi's net worth was over seven hundred million dollars? Lexi wanted to be herself, but she also didn't want Derek to think that she was just a rich tourist, because she wasn't—she was so much more than the sum of her investments, and she was here to stay. With difficulty, she set the photo back on the table and looked again at her sea turtle picture. "I heard that Ke'e Beach is a good place to watch the sea turtles."

"Poipu is nice, too," Derek said. "It's not far from here. A bit more rocky, but there is a great area next to the Beach House restaurant that always has turtles and fish."

Lexi pulled her bottom lip through her teeth. "I'm a strong swimmer. Do you think snorkeling's something that I could figure out on my own?"

"I could teach you," Derek offered. "I've lived here for a couple years, and I go out at least once a week. I'd like to get a few more shots tomorrow. What do you think?"

She nearly took a step back. She'd barely met Derek, and he was already asking to spend time with her. Her gut reaction was to turn him away. But wait . . . he didn't know who she was or that she was a multimillionaire. Derek wasn't after her money. A thrill shot through Lexi when she realized he would never have to know. She could get to know him—or anyone on this island—without all of her money trailing along like excess baggage. Lexi pressed her lips together, considering his open face. The impact of his offer reminded her of why she'd decided to come to Kauai. She leaned forward and smiled. "Are you sure? It might be hard for you to get any good pictures if I'm sucking the ocean through my breathing tube."

Derek laughed. "I think I'm a pretty good teacher. So do you want to meet at Ke'e Beach on the north shore?"

"Maybe?" Lexi drew her sandaled foot along the grass, letting the blades tickle her toes.

"Or we could meet here, and we can ride up together?"

Lexi liked how Derek wasn't trying to get personal too quickly by asking to pick her up at her house. "Do you live close to here?"

He pointed a thumb over his shoulder. "Just a few blocks away."

Again she hesitated, but Derek waited patiently, no flicker of frustration on his face. She swallowed and took a step forward. "I live in Princeville, so I'll meet you at the beach."

He nodded. "Do you know where to rent some gear?"

"Actually, I bought some in the hopes that I could figure it out."

"Sounds like you're ready, then. If you want to swim with the turtles, it's best to go early. Can you be there by seven in the morning?"

"Yep. The birds around here make sure everyone is up early."

"Especially the roosters." Derek chuckled and held out a business card. "Here's my number. If you have any questions, give me a call."

"Thanks." Lexi pocketed the card, again grateful at how easygoing Derek was. He hadn't pressed her for her phone number or address. What a nice change from the speed-dating types who sought her out at every business function. "And thanks for sharing your talents. I'm glad you were here."

Derek looked down with a half smile and murmured, "Me, too."

Lexi meandered back through a few booths, all the time wishing she could be bold and go back and talk to Derek about snorkeling, photography, or anything. When she glanced back to find him watching her, she smiled. Tomorrow morning seemed like a very long time away for a snorkeling lesson with the good-looking photographer.

25

Chapter 4

When Lexi woke up at five o'clock Saturday morning, she blamed it on Chicago, not a handsome photographer. Lexi unpacked another suitcase containing most of the toiletries she needed to finish setting up in her bathroom. After that she moved to the kitchen, admiring the white cabinets with teal handles that matched the backsplash—a mosaic of square tiles in teal, white quartz, and gray. The kitchen boasted a modern look that flowed throughout the house. Lexi took a moment to admire the home . . . her home.

Shawn had found the home, newly remodeled, mostly furnished, and two hours on the market. For that, Lexi would always be grateful. Lexi shook her head. She needed to stop thinking about Shawn and his attempt to form a serious relationship with her. She liked him, and at one time she'd experienced feelings for him during what she defined as stressful, mind-numbing work that left her defenses down. Shawn was handsome in a preppy sort of way and a good friend of Jordan's, but even Lexi's brother couldn't convince her to stay and give Shawn or Burke Enterprises any more chances.

Lexi wiped off the kitchen counter, trying to wipe Chicago from her thoughts. She gathered her beach bag and snorkeling gear and loaded up her Jeep. It was barely six-thirty and the morning was quiet, save for the wildlife chattering in the trees. The air smelled faintly of plumeria, rain, and the red dirt on the roadside. Lexi rolled down her window and let the breeze tickle the tendrils of hair curling around her neck. Traffic was light, almost nonexistent compared to Chicago.

Ke'e Beach, in Haena State Park, was at the end of the highway; the road ended at the sand as though even Kauai knew that this was Lexi's destination. She found a parking spot off the grassy shoulder and walked toward the constant rush of the ocean waves that called to her, drowning out the butterflies in her stomach.

Lexi took off her flip-flops and tucked them into her bag as the sand grew deeper. She strolled along the shore, admiring both the ocean and the trees behind her. Many of the roots were exposed, creating an odd-looking bramble of smooth red bones jutting from the grassy bank and trailing towards the finer sand of the beach.

"Aloha, Lexi."

She turned to see Derek walking toward her, lugging a large bag of his own, probably filled with his photography gear. "Aloha." Lexi admired Derek's dark green board shorts, tight black swim shirt, and tanned bare feet. The messy, spiked look of his coarse dark hair set off the perfect contour of his dark eyebrows. *Yummy* was the thought that flitted through Lexi's mind before she snapped out of the laser scrutiny of her sexy snorkeling teacher.

Derek was holding back a laugh as he waited for Lexie to snap out of her reverie. "I forgot to remind you about a rash guard. It helps you stay warm and keeps your back from getting sunburnt." Derek held up a green swim shirt with his Fuse logo on it.

Grateful for the distraction, Lexi stepped forward, taking the silky shirt. "Thanks. I won't confess that I feel like a fish out of water here . . . this is called a rash guard?"

"Fair enough. I won't confess that I ate cold pizza for breakfast this morning."

Lexi laughed and pointed to herself. "Granola bar and yogurt. My fridge needs help."

"So you really did just move here?"

"Yeah, I stopped by the grocery store my first day here to grab a few essentials. I got lost twice already, but I think I'm figuring things out now."

"Or at least your GPS has been updated," Derek teased.

"Who needs GPS? I have pomaika'i." She turned to survey the water. "So where's the best place to snorkel?"

"You do have good luck." Derek chuckled and pointed to a spot where the ocean crashed against a rugged-looking mountain. "Near the edge of the reef is where the turtles are, with tons more fish on the other side, but we won't start there. I like to keep an eye on the water, make sure it's calm enough; otherwise it isn't safe to go outside the reef. The waves are wilder on the north shore."

Lexi was about to ask why he thought a beach on the north shore was a good place to learn to snorkel when he motioned to a shallow pool in front of them. "The reef creates sort of a swimming hole, and in an hour or so, this beach will be absolutely crawling. Right now the water's calm, and this is an excellent place to try on your gear. C'mon, I'll show you."

"I'm really excited, but nervous, too. I hope I don't choke on salt water," Lexi said as she trudged through the sand to the water's edge.

"I always recommend not drinking the ocean." Derek set his bag on the sand with a wink. Lexi put her bag down next to his, and they both pulled out snorkeling gear. "Now, this next part might not be for city girls, but I'm too cheap for anti-fog spray." Derek spit right into his mask, rubbed it around with his fingers, and then rinsed it in the saltwater.

Lexi grimaced. Why didn't anyone tell her about anti-fog spray? Now she would have to spit in front of a guy so good-looking, he even looked hot defogging his snorkeling mask. Lexi's mouth suddenly went dry; she swallowed and spit a tiny amount into the mask.

"Here, let me help you." Derek took the mask, wiped around the lens, and dipped it in the water. "See, now you can really say you're not a tourist."

"If that's what it takes." Lexi gripped the mask, knowing she was going to look like a complete dork.

Derek slipped his mask on easily and gave her a thumbs-up. "Yes. Snorkeling is not a sport for the vain, because everyone looks funny in this getup. Care to join me?"

With his nose blocked, he sounded funny, too. Lexi laughed and some of the tension eased from her body. Grateful that she'd taken the time to try on her snorkeling mask at home so she wouldn't look completely inept, she blew out a breath and pulled on her mask feeling like an awkward teenager again. When she looked up at Derek wearing his mask, waiting to teach her how to snorkel and still looking hot, she bit the mouthpiece hard and reminded herself to pay attention.

Derek gave her a few pointers about sucking in air through her nose to provide a tight suction on her face which caused the mask to dig into her cheeks. Then they strapped on their flippers and waded backwards until the water hit Lexi's waist.

"This is colder than I thought!" Lexi shrieked as a small wave pushed the water level above her belly button. She shivered.

"Once the sun moves out from the clouds, it'll feel a lot better." Derek pointed to a few rays of light streaking above the trees that surrounded the beach. "A wetsuit comes in handy if you're going to be out longer than an hour, but I thought we'd just spend a little time this morning to get you started, see how you like it."

Lexi shivered again. "Okay, I'm ready."

"Kneel down here and put your face in the water. You don't even need to worry about breathing this first time. Just test that your seal is tight so you don't get salt water in your eyes."

Lexi knelt down just as another wave rolled toward the shore. The water tugged her forward and Derek grabbed her hand to steady her. The sand shifted under her knees, and she gripped his fingers tightly, dunking her face into the water.

Thrust into a different world, Lexi widened her eyes as the silent layer of water just below the surface filled her ears. She scooped up a handful of sand, the grains drifting away with the tide. Derek squeezed her fingers, and she turned to see his head also underneath the water. She squeezed back and enjoyed the warm buzz of adrenaline surging through her body. The mouthpiece was snug against her lips, so she took one careful breath, hearing the hollow tube vibrate with air against the side of her head. She breathed in and out once more and then lifted her face out of the water, surprised at how a couple inches felt like she had been immersed in the ocean.

She pulled the mouthpiece out as Derek lifted his head. "I did it! I took a breath. Did I just snorkel?"

Derek chuckled, and his laugh whistled through his breathing tube. He moved it aside. "Great work for your first try. Now let's swim a little farther out, and we'll just float on top of the water. You can lift your head up anytime you get nervous. I think you'll see a few fish closer to the reef."

Lexi held on to him as they swam further toward the Ke'e reef. Her fingers tingled with his touch. Even though she knew Derek only held her hand to steady her, she enjoyed the strength in his grip. The shoreline fell away gradually until the water reached Lexi's armpits.

"This looks like a good place. You ready?" Derek lifted his eyebrows and smiled.

When he smiled like that, revealing white, even teeth and a full bottom lip, the ocean felt ten degrees warmer. Lexi nodded and adjusted her mask. "Do I need to swim or tread water as we go farther out?"

"Nope," Derek answered. "It doesn't matter how deep the water is for snorkeling, because you're floating on the surface."

Lexi swayed with the constant roll of the waves. "Are you sure I won't sink?"

"Here, watch me." He put in his mouthpiece and ducked into the water. A second later, his body popped back up, floating still and golden with the sun reflecting off the waves. His calves were toned and lean. At first glance, Lexi had guessed he was Hawaiian, but the more she considered him, the less certain she was that he was a native to Hawaii. He'd mentioned living in Kauai for a couple years. His head popped back up. "See? Now it's your turn."

Lexi didn't tell him that she'd been too busy admiring his physique to focus on how she would mimic his floating posture. With the constant motion of the water, the fish swimming below her, and the thoughts of turtles swimming within reach, Lexi's insides tightened up into a ball of nerves. "You won't let me get washed out to sea, right?"

Derek laughed, and the sound was an elixir for the tightness that had crept into Lexi's shoulders. She blew out a breath, and put her head in the water. For one second, all was dark, and then she remembered to open her eyes. An entire world waited right under the surface. A black-and-yellow fish darted by, and she gasped. The sound in her tube jolted her brain, reminding her to suck in a breath. Her inhale echoed in the tube, and she glanced to the side to see Derek floating right next to her. She started to smile, but then remembered her mouthpiece and bit down.

A school of silver-and-blue fish darted past, and Lexi reached out in front of her. The fish were farther away than they appeared. The world just below the surface held every shade of blue, from almost white down to the cobalt blue near the sand. Rays of sunlight skimmed the surface and filled Lexi's soul with joy in this moment of quiet peace where everything moved at the pace God intended. She marveled at the rocks with bits of coral, the fish darting in and out, the sand shifting along the bottom of the ocean. Everything so simple, yet so beautiful.

Derek took her hand, and she turned slowly to meet his eyes. He gave her a thumbs-up. She nodded and returned the signal, wondering if he could sense what she was experiencing as the power of the moment intensified. He pointed in front of him and gave her a little tug. With a kick of her flippers, she followed, gripping his hand tightly. Her heart pounded, every beat more exhilarating than the one before, as she watched a large rainbow-colored fish duck behind a rock.

One part of her consciousness focused on the glorious world around her, and the other part was aware of every movement of Derek's fingertips as he gently guided her forward. She noticed a black-and-white fish glide past a piece of seaweed tangled around a rock; she also noticed the muscles in Derek's forearms, the way his broad shoulders filled out his shirt. He turned back, and Lexi was grateful for the bulky mask—he didn't know she was gawking at him instead of the fish.

Suddenly, he kicked his flippers and was at her side, pointing behind her. She swiveled and saw a sea turtle diving down from the surface. Derek put his hand on the small of her back and propelled her forward, in pursuit of the turtle. Lexi barely had to kick her feet; they must have been moving with the current for how quickly the rocks and schools of fish came in and out of focus.

Squeezing her hand, Derek came to a stop and pointed again. Three more turtles swam nearer to the surface and a fourth skidded along the bottom of the ocean. Lexi hung there, suspended between water and air by a few inches, and took in the scene before her. The turtles were absolutely delightful to watch as their flippers moved them gracefully through the water. The bulky shells confounded her because it seemed like the turtles shouldn't be able to flip, dive, and move so quickly through the water. There was so much life around her in the wild ocean, and Lexi wanted to soak it all in. She wanted to be like those turtles and surprise everyone, but mostly herself, with an ability to relax and enjoy life like she'd never been able to before. She was living out a dream, and she didn't want to wake up.

Derek motioned upwards, and Lexi lifted her head out of the water. The rush of sound, a stark contrast to the silence just below them, surrounded her, leaving her slightly disoriented. Derek let go of her hand to remove his breathing tube. "It makes you feel like you're part of two worlds, doesn't it?"

"Yeah, that's exactly how I feel right now. Those turtles were so neat. I can't believe that we just swam with sea turtles!" Lexi laughed, throwing her head back.

Derek joined her laughter, pushing his mask up on his head. "I'm glad I got to make this memory with you."

Lexi pulled her mask down around her neck. She reached out and touched his arm. "Me, too."

Derek glanced at her hand and then looked at her with an intensity that made her knees feel weak. His eyes looked lighter today under the sunshine. Lexi thought she saw flecks of gold interspersed with the brown. "You've been working hard for a long time, haven't you?" His voice was quiet and his question was spot on.

Lexi sighed. "Too long. It's like I don't even know how to relax anymore. I feel like a naughty kid skipping school."

Derek chuckled. "It took some time getting used to island life, and some of my buddies still razz me about working too hard, but I think I've found a pace that I like."

They floated in the water close to each other, yet not close enough. Lexi wanted to touch him, hold his hand, and maybe be wrapped in those strong arms. She shook her head. *Whoa, where did that come from?* Maybe she was suffering from sunstroke, even though it was barely eight o'clock, and the sun kept hiding behind the clouds casting shadows over the water. She glanced at Derek's bronzed skin and dark hair, water droplets glistening on the sexy scruff lining his jaw. Yes, it was sunstroke. That was it.

She cleared her throat and her mind, remembering that this guy was just teaching her how to snorkel. He was a Good Samaritan of sorts. "Do you need to take some photos? I hope I didn't take up too much of your time."

"Nah, I was out past the reef at six, and I got some great shots. I got here early and saw how calm it was and decided to take advantage of nature's gift to this humble photographer."

Lexi wanted to ask him all about his photos. She hesitated, and then decided it was time to get out of her shell. "I'd love to see some of those pictures and check out your camera, if you wouldn't mind showing me."

Derek's mouth turned up in that easy smile, and he nodded. "Okay, sure. Do you want to snorkel for a few more minutes as we make our way back to shore?"

"Definitely." Lexi busied herself with her mask and breathing tube. She needed to put her head underwater before she ended up asking Derek out on a date.

They swam around the reef, and Derek pointed out more turtles and brightly colored fish. The marine life was unlike anything Lexi had imagined or could describe. She would have to call her brother and tell him he needed to take a vacation. Lexi kicked lightly with her flippers and followed Derek's lead as he swam close to the reef and pointed at a bright pink piece of coral on the ledge. Lexi admired the rainbow of colors on display and watched another school of fish jet by.

The current shifted, and the rocks that had seemed so far away suddenly loomed close. She put her hands out in front of her, but then remembered the strict commands she'd heard about not touching coral. Kicking backwards, she fought against another wave pushing into the reef. She panicked and opened her mouth to cry out, the salty taste of the ocean reminding her to keep her lips closed. Derek grabbed her around the middle and hauled her away from the reef. His arms were as strong and confident as she'd thought they'd be. She relaxed, thinking she could snorkel like this all day long. To her disappointment, he shifted his hold to her hand and continued to swim forward.

She lifted her head out of the water, and Derek followed. "Sorry about that. The tide is changing. It's time to get back inside the reef. Are you okay?"

"Yeah, I didn't know what was happening. I thought I was going to be a rock sandwich."

Derek shook his head. "I wouldn't let that happen. Follow me, and we'll get back to the beach. I'm sorry I didn't get you out of there before the tide changed. It's kind of scary if you don't know what to expect."

"Okay." There wasn't time to say more, because Derek went back underwater. The change in the rolling motion of the waves was scary, and her heart beat in her throat. She focused on the feel of Derek's palm against hers as she swam beside him.

Once they were back inside the swimming hole, Derek slowed his pace and pointed out more fish. He didn't tell her not to be scared, or laugh off her worries—he'd apologized and told her he would protect her. He was giving her the chance to feel comfortable and enjoy the water like she had at first so she wouldn't be afraid to go back out. Instead of judgment, Derek offered understanding. As her heart rate decreased, she thought about the scenario and realized she probably hadn't been in any real danger.

Derek's genuine kindness, the way he took her hand in his, and that brilliant smile made Lexi's heart skip a beat and take off running again. She watched a blue-and-yellow fish swim in front of her and gripped his hand, wondering if he could feel the thrum of energy in her fingertips.

Chapter 5

Once they reached the shore, Derek took off his rash guard and squeezed the excess water out of the shirt. He toweled off, trying not to watch Lexi do the same. The hot-pink paint on her toenails matched her pink-and-green bikini, which he'd reluctantly helped her cover up with his extra rash guard. She'd done great for her first time snorkeling. The edges of her mouth kept turning up in a smile, so hopefully that meant she was happy with the lesson she'd had despite the few moments of fear.

"Our gear is over there." Derek pointed a few hundred yards away.

"I feel lost after being underwater."

"It takes a few minutes to get your bearings, but I always mark my spot by a certain tree or something so I know where to head." He touched her shoulder to turn her toward their bags in the sand. She stiffened slightly, and then relaxed under his touch, her skin warm and inviting. He quickly moved his hand, afraid that maybe he'd crossed a line.

"It's so beautiful," she said. "Makes me want to sit here all day and stare at the ocean."

"It's one of those things that will hold your interest for a lifetime." He glanced away from her face before she caught him staring.

As they walked up the beach, he noticed how Lexi kept watching the waves, looking wistful. He was intrigued by Lexi. She hadn't shared much about herself or why she was here on this island, but the way she'd tensed when he touched her shoulders spoke of too much stress for too long. He wondered if she'd last. He'd seen it before: people came to Kauai to get away from it all, but after a few weeks they were restless and looking for ways to fill the void that they'd carried with them all along. He wanted to ask her out on a date, but he didn't want to get his heart tangled up with someone who would be hopping to another island in a month. And Lexi was the type of woman who could definitely tangle up his heart.

"I'm excited to see if I recognize any of the fish in your pictures now that I've been on my first snorkeling adventure," Lexi said.

She sounded genuinely interested, so when they reached their bags, Derek took out his camera, scrolling through a few of the shots from that morning. Lexi sat next to him on the sand, her shoulder brushing his as she leaned in to look at the screen on his camera. He pulled up several shots of the sea turtles playing in the water outside the reef, knowing she was partial to them.

"I could watch them for hours," Lexi said. "I mean, I've already spent a few doing that when I should have been unpacking, but it's addictive. I never thought something as simple as a sea turtle would make me feel so, so . . ."

"At ease? Joy and excitement wrapped together?" Derek supplied.

Lexi brightened and pointed at a group of turtles on his camera. "Yes. I feel like a little girl at the zoo. Only now I'm not just visiting—I live here."

"This island will keep surprising you if you give it a chance." Derek found himself grinning at Lexi as he talked about Kauai. His heart clenched when he considered his thoughts from earlier. He hoped Lexi would last on the island.

"Oh, I like that one." Lexi pointed at two turtles he'd photographed underwater.

Derek zoomed in a couple notches. "These two look like they are just about to kiss."

"Now that's romantic."

He scoffed. "Yeah, two bumpy, wrinkled turtles."

"I'm serious. I love the way you captured them in that tiny moment where they appear to be looking at each other, like they know each other's souls." Lexi's voice trailed off, and she ducked her head.

Derek turned to her, noticing how her upper lip formed a perfect bow shape. As a photographer, he noticed fine details all the time, but a flash of heat ran through his middle as he wondered how it would feel to kiss her. He cleared his throat and looked back at the turtles. "You're right. Now if you'd come and talk about my pictures like that at the street fair . . ."

Lexi laughed. "Print that one up in several different sizes. I bet you'll sell them all in the first hour."

He liked the glint of a dare in her eyes. "You think so, huh? Care to wager on that?"

She scooped up a handful of sand and let it sift through her fingers. "Okay, if you don't sell out I'll buy you a mahi-mahi dinner. But if you do, then you owe me."

Derek held out his hand. "You're on."

She grinned and shook it. Derek found himself smiling almost as big as Pika did when he caught the perfect wave surfing. That thought knocked Lexi out of his brain, and he glanced at his watch. "Man, I didn't realize it was already nine o'clock. I'd better get to work."

"Oh, I thought you were 'at work.'" Lexi pointed at his camera.

Derek carefully packed up and zipped his bag. "My friend Pika sells coconuts at the base of the hiking trail right over there." He pointed at the mountain rising up beyond the lifeguard tower. "I'll be chopping for the rest of the day because he's shorthanded."

"Chopping?"

"Haven't you had a coconut water yet?"

"The kind in the little box with the straw? Yeah, I picked a few up in the airport."

Derek wrinkled his nose. "No way. The kind *in* the coconut with the straw."

Lexi furrowed her brow. "I thought coconuts had milk inside?"

Derek smiled and shook his head. "Now, see, I knew you were a tourist." He laughed when Lexi huffed. "Coconuts have liquid inside—their water. It's full of vitamins and minerals that are especially great for hydrating after a long hike. If you want coconut milk, you have to make that by grinding up the coconut and squeezing out the pulp."

Lexi jumped to her feet. "Can I see? That sounds so cool."

Derek stood next to her and shouldered his bag. She probably wouldn't be impressed when she saw the gritty work it took to open the coconuts, but she hadn't balked at spitting in her mask, so she should be fine. "Okay, but I'll warn you now: don't believe anything that Pika says."

"Got it." Lexi nodded, and then tilted her head. "He's your friend, though, right?"

Derek laughed. "Yep, best friend that treats me like a little brother every chance he gets."

"Should be interesting." Lexi quickened her step.

For a moment, Derek wondered if maybe it wasn't a good idea for Lexi to meet his rough-around-the-edges friend. Pika liked to make fun of tourists even though they made his job possible.

They passed the sign for the Kalalau Trail and Lexi grabbed his arm. "Oh, this is the hike I read about in my guidebook!" Lexi clapped and gazed upwards.

"Do you like hiking?" Derek followed her gaze, his skin tingling where she'd touched his arm.

"I'm from Chicago, so not much hiking there, but I love exploring, and I want to get to know this island."

It was the perfect excuse to ask her out. Derek had held back earlier, and because of Lexi's dare that he turned into a wager, they would be seeing each other again. But the street fair didn't take place for almost another week. He didn't want to wait that long to see the sparkle in Lexi's green eyes. He pointed at the mountain and then at her. "Would you like to go Monday morning?"

Lexi turned to him with a smile. She nibbled the inside of her cheek as she considered his offer, probably noting the significance of them doing something together again so soon. Her shoulders rose and fell as she took in a breath. "I would love that. What's the best time to start?"

"Any time, but how about seven again? The trail is pretty quiet that time of day, and Pika will probably be here chopping coconuts by the time we get back."

"So you can go to work, right?"

Derek shrugged. "Unless something better comes up before that."

"I think that sounds like a perfect way to start the week."

"Me, too." Derek's heart thrummed in his chest, and he was acutely aware of Lexi walking close to his side.

They continued walking toward Pika's beat-up red pickup. The tailgate was down, and Pika stood in the center swinging his machete with precise strokes while tourists watched him. It only took a few chops to remove the outer shell of the coconut, the skins piled up in the back of the pickup behind Pika. He hefted the milky white coconut to a pile and started on another one. Pika's mother, Kima, bent over a cooler and retrieved a coconut. Her eyes nearly disappeared in the folds of wrinkles as she gave the fresh coconut to an older gentleman.

"Is that your friend?" Lexi asked.

Derek nodded. Pika wore a tank top and shorts, and his thighs were probably as big around as Lexi's waist. Derek looked at Lexi out of the corner of his eye to see if she was ogling Pika like so many of the women who stopped here tended to do. He breathed a sigh of relief as she watched Kima handing out coconuts. He and Pika had vied for more than one girl's attention the past few years. They usually went for the chiseled islander heaving a machete, not the lanky photographer beside him.

Derek steered Lexi toward Kima. "Hey, *makuahine*, how about one of those coconuts for my friend, Lexi?"

Kima straightened and reached her arms out to hug Derek. "So good of you to come and help Pika. He's chopping fast, but so many people already today." She released Derek and moved to Lexi. "Oh, your *beautiful* friend. If you want to keep your *wahine*, give the proper introduction."

Derek's face burned at Kima calling Lexi his "woman." He should be used to Kima's teasing about him finding a woman by now, but he was self-conscious today, like Lexi meant more than the other girls he'd brought around—not that there had been many. "Lexi, this is Pika's mother, Kima." He glanced at Lexi, and she was smiling, her face tinged red as well.

She held out her hand. "Aloha, I'm Lexi Burke. I just moved to Princeville, and I have to say that your island is the beautiful thing."

Kima waved off Lexi's hand and embraced her. "Mahalo nui loa. I say, thank you very much."

Derek saw a break in the line of people. Any minute, Pika would stop chopping and start hollering; then he'd stop working altogether when he saw Lexi. Derek grabbed a coconut out of the cooler and put a straw in the center. He handed it to Lexi with a smile. "Lexi's never had fresh coconut water before, and I told her this is the place to try it."

Lexi took the coconut and sipped the straw tentatively. She swallowed with a puzzled expression. "It's good, not what I expected at all. Thank you."

Kima patted her cheek. "It's good for your skin and your heart." She glanced at Derek, but he pretended not to notice. Kima was anything but subtle when it came to matchmaking.

"I'd better get chopping," Derek said. "Enjoy your coconut."

"Thank you, I will." Lexi put her hand on his arm. "Thanks for the wonderful morning. I hope you have a lot of success today."

"Saturdays are crazy busy, so I'm sure we will, and I won't be able to lift my arms tomorrow." He covered her hand with his and smiled. "See you later."

Derek stowed his gear and then stepped toward the pickup, hopping up next to Pika.

"Hey, bro, finally decided to let the girl drink her coconut in peace? Thought you'd never get up here," Pika said.

Derek laughed. Pika thought he was just flirting with one of the customers. Time for him to stake his claim if he wanted any chance of getting to know Lexi without Pika interfering. "That's Lexi. She moved to the island, and I taught her how to snorkel this morning."

Pika stopped and lifted his chin. "She like you?"

Derek shrugged. "She's a nice girl. She likes my photos."

Pika smiled wide and smacked Derek across the back. "She must have been looking at pictures of me, then."

Derek shook his head. "Could have been, but she thought they were turtles."

Both of them laughed, and Pika started chopping again. Derek pushed aside the husks, clearing a space for him to work. He was grateful that Lexi wouldn't have to endure Pika's "charm."

"My uncle's bringing another load after noon." Pika grunted as he rolled another coconut into place. "It's gonna be a big day."

"Hand me that machete." Derek stretched his arms over his head, watching Lexi talk with Kima before walking back down toward the beach. He moved into position and chopped the green from the coconut, revealing the rough, white flesh. When he and Pika were in the zone, they could chop four coconuts per minute. His mind was already busy retracing every moment he and Lexi had shared that morning.

It wasn't until after Lexi left that Derek realized he still didn't have her number. He had wanted to give her space and time to trust him at first, but now he wished he'd been bold. He brought his machete down hard on the next coconut. He'd just have to pray that she showed up Monday morning.

About an hour later, Derek stopped for a short break. He stretched his shoulders and ate a few mouthfuls of coconut flesh from one of the fruits that had split open. His phone vibrated with a text, and he pulled it out of his pocket and slid his finger across the screen.

Thanks so much for teaching me how to snorkel! And teaching me about coconuts! You have my number now. ☺

One side of Derek's mouth lifted, and he pocketed his phone. Lexi had kept the business card with his number he'd given her last night, and she'd reached out. He'd wait until later to reply—Pika would never let him hear the end of it otherwise.

Chapter 6

Lexi's cheeks hurt from smiling by the time she walked through her front door. Derek had been featured in at least every other thought all the way home. She'd turned back to watch him chop coconuts while he talked with Pika. The Polynesian man was stunning with his dark skin, bulging muscles, and quick strikes of the machete, but Lexi's eyes were drawn to Derek. He carried himself with an ease and agility that belied the strength she'd felt when he'd pulled her away from the rocks that morning. A thrill zinged through her when she remembered the feel of his hands around her waist.

It was time to get her mind occupied with something besides Derek.

She pushed herself to unpack the remaining boxes and made a checklist of things she would need in her new living space. The home was sparsely furnished, but what she really needed was a comfortable overstuffed chair. She could sit in front of the window off the kitchen that overlooked the ocean and enjoy the view on a stormy day.

After lunch, which consisted of a grilled ham-and-cheese sandwich, Lexi walked around her house trying to decide what to do. She stubbed her toe on the box of art supplies she'd partially unpacked, but instead of cursing it, she smiled. The new stretched canvas she'd purchased leaned against the wall in her bedroom, tempting her with possibilities. Lexi stretched her arms over her head and rolled her shoulders back. She found the bag of new supplies and stepped outside.

For the next twenty minutes she worked to create an artist's cove on her balcony with a makeshift easel made from two long planks she found in her backyard. The list of essential items doubled as Lexi thought of all the things she needed to order online to complete her nook of creativity. Finally, she settled in with a large, flat brush and a cerulean blue oil paint. She primed the canvas and stood back to stare at the beginnings of something that whispered to her soul; a soul that had been caged too long and was hungry for this new life.

Oils were arrayed like a rainbow next to her canvas. In college, her professor had been a starving artist and insisted on teaching his students how to mix colors to make every shade with a handful of oils. Lexi ran her fingers over the row of tubes, grateful that she didn't have to worry about painting with a budget of only six basic colors.

She switched brushes and played around with raw sienna, blending it to color the beach in her painting, thinking of how her brother Jordan would love the scene from her balcony. Lexi concentrated on her painting and worked to create the fine line between sand and surf, but her mind kept straying to Jordan and how much she missed him.

He'd kept his word and given her time and space to get settled in Kauai. Her brother's eyes had brimmed with tears when she'd given him her final answer—she wouldn't be returning to Burke Enterprises. The business would experience hiccups in her absence, but she doubted that was the reason Jordan had shown a wide arc of emotions when she left.

When Jordan dropped her off at the airport, she'd hugged him and said, "I love you, Jordy, but I need at least a week before we talk. Otherwise, I know you'll guilt-trip me into coming back before I even have a chance to get settled."

Jordan had hesitated before ruffling her hair. "You have my number. I'll wait until you call me. I'm sorry you've been so unhappy here." His sincerity twisted like a knife in Lexi's gut, and it took everything she had to walk away from the empire that she and her brother had built together. She hated that he blamed himself for her unhappiness when he'd given her so much. Jordy was the best of big brothers. He took her leaving personally, but Lexi hoped to convince him of her gratitude for the chance he'd given her to work with him and partner the company—without strings.

Lexi groaned. She couldn't get the sand to look right, and she doubted she'd make any progress at all until she cleared the emotional air with Jordan. She set her brush down, fished out her phone, and dialed Chicago.

His assistant answered, and a flash of doubt passed through Lexi as she thought of her own assistant. She wondered if Shawn had garnered the position he'd been vying for, but she wouldn't ask about him.

After a couple minutes, Jordan came on the line. "Lexi, is this really you?"

"Yep, I figured you'd be up and working instead of sleeping."

Jordan chuckled. "One of these days I'll try one of those forty-hour weeks for a change. I hear they're pretty tough."

Lexi laughed. Her brother had consistently worked sixty- to eighty-hour weeks for the last five years. Her shoulders tightened when she thought about how many times she'd matched his timesheet. A gust of salty ocean wind blew across her balcony, and she sighed. "I don't miss that, you know. I didn't realize how drained I was until I came here. I think I was on my last piston."

"That's my fault, Lex. I shouldn't have worked you so hard." Jordan's voice was regretful.

"No, I jumped right in with you. I loved the challenge, the success, that drive that I couldn't turn off—but it's not everything."

"You did the right thing, sis. I know Mom and Dad would be proud of you." Jordan might not agree with her statement, but at least he agreed with her choice.

Lexi wished for a moment that she could convince her brother to slow down and experience life, but she wasn't qualified to do that yet. One week in Kauai was tourism, a short vacation. She sat up straighter, determined to support Jordan. "They'd be proud of both of us. I bet Dad is up in heaven shaking his head, trying to fathom that we're worth a billion dollars together."

"About that, Lex." Jordan cleared his throat. "Do you remember those factories we invested in near Hong Kong?"

"Yeah, there were six in Guangzhou and four in Dongguan, right?" Lexi wondered what Jordan was about to say. His tone was light, so it must not be bad news.

"You haven't lost that money-making memory yet. Well, we have some interested buyers, and I've decided to take your advice and sell off some of our stress load. Are you still okay with that?"

"Most definitely. That would be terrific, but are they really worth much?" Lexi asked.

Jordan cleared his throat again. "I think they might be worth more than we originally thought."

"Well, go for it. I can't believe it took my moving half a world away for you to see reason," she teased.

"I've missed you, sis. It's been just you and me for a while now."

"Maybe it's time to open your heart and let someone else in."

"What's that? I guess I have another meeting, Lexi. But hey—I wondered if you could skype next week about the Falzon account."

Lexi smiled. She knew exactly what Jordan was doing: deftly changing the subject. And if she didn't get the hint, he'd added the bombshell invite to re-enter the biggest and most stressful account the Burke Enterprises had ever procured. A bird called from the tree to the left of her balcony, and Lexi looked at her canvas from a different angle. An idea popped into her head to add more texture to the sand. Her fingers itched to try it out. "Hmm, I think I'll pass. While you're selling those companies, get rid of Falzon, too."

"No problem. I'll just flush a few mil down the toilet for fun."

They'd both hit their marks, and now it was time to wrap up before she said something she shouldn't. "Look, I'd better go now before my paint dries, but I just wanted to tell you I love you and thanks for supporting me."

"Wait, you're painting? Who are you, and what did you do with my sister?"

"I'll text you my work in progress."

"I love you, too. You're a great example to me."

It took a few minutes to immerse herself in the painting after talking to Jordan, but soon she was sweeping brushstrokes across the blue ocean expanse that rolled in its ever-changing colors and forms a hundred yards from her house.

There was a particular color of aquamarine with a tinge of Payne's gray that she wanted to get just right for a wave cresting in the distance. The incoming tide made her think of her parents, and emotions that she'd dealt with long ago bubbled to the surface. Four and a half years ago, Jordan and Lexi's parents were killed in a head-on collision with a cement truck. They were on their way home from a movie, and Lexi's mom, Shalice, had just texted her that she should go see it. Lexi didn't remember the movie now, but she remembered how the disbelief and emptiness overtook her when she learned they had been killed. The shock intensified when Jordan and Lexi were contacted by an attorney to go over the life insurance policies for twenty-five million dollars on each of their parents. Suddenly, Jordan and Lexi were multimillionaire orphans.

Jordan had already started Burke Enterprises—working ninety-hour weeks, flying back and forth to China—and it was a success. When he suggested that they invest their money into his business and that Lexi should come work for him and become a partner in Burke Enterprises, it seemed like the only thing that made sense in her crazy, turned-upside-down world.

After a couple of years working with Jordan, she had discovered that being a millionaire didn't mean you could sleep in and order crumpets and tea—at least not if Jordan was your brother. Burke Enterprises continued to grow, providing jobs for thousands of Chinese workers as well as hundreds in the States at their home offices in Chicago. She had dealt with anxiety, stress, and apathy for far too long before finally calling it quits.

Lexi tightened her grip on the paintbrush. She wouldn't go back to that life. If only she could convince Jordan to come for a visit—maybe he would see there was more to life than work.

Chapter 7

ika and Derek made over six hundred dollars on Saturday, and while Derek was carefully counting out his money Sunday morning, Pika hit the surf to celebrate. "I'll meet you at one o'clock. Hopefully Jefe will have run out of coconuts by then."

Derek sighed, but he knew he'd be back on that truck chopping his guts out; the money was too good to pass up. He massaged his right shoulder, wincing at the tenderness from chopping for six hours. He wondered what Lexi did for work. She hadn't mentioned anything so far, except that she'd overtaxed her reserves before moving to Kauai. The corporate grind would probably take some time to recover from—not that he would know. He kept thinking of questions he wanted to ask Lexi, and now that he had her number, he could. He didn't want to come across as needy, though, so he left his phone alone.

Derek slung his camera bag over his head and drove to Waimea Canyon. He'd had a couple people ask about photos of Kauai's own Grand Canyon at the last street fair. Maybe getting in some nice shots of the reds and greens rippling across the dry scene would keep his mind off Lexi.

Monday morning, Derek's muscles protested from the weekend, but his mind was clear and full of anticipation to see Lexi. With money problems under control for another month, everything looked brighter on the island as he drove up to Ke'e Beach. He parked his car, grinning when Lexi texted him that she was waiting by the sign for the trail. She was a few hundred yards away, and she was here to see him. Well, here to see the sights, but she was *with* him, and that was good enough for now. Even though he'd tried to humbly tell himself that he was just showing her the island, the way his heart rose every time he thought of her was proof that it was more than sightseeing to him.

He quickened his step and skirted between the trees. Lexi's hair hung in a loose braid halfway down her back. She wore a lime-green racerback tank top and blue athletic pants that were cropped at her calves, which were quite shapely. She turned and caught his eye, her cheeks lifting in a grin. He waved, and she held up one hand with fluttering fingers. She seemed different, lighter somehow, with a glow of happiness. Derek hoped it was partly because of him, but he knew that Hawaii was probably responsible.

"Aloha," he said when he reached her side. "You ready for this?"

He didn't think it was possible, but her grin widened. "I've been ready for this my whole life. I just didn't know it until last week."

"Now that's enthusiasm." Derek chuckled. He put his hand on the small of her back, guiding her toward the trailhead. "That's Pika's main competitor right there." Derek pointed to a pickup so covered in rust spots that the remaining bits of blue paint were more like accents to the dark brown stains.

"Not too much different from Pika's truck, right?"

"Yeah, but Jefe is lazy. He only brings enough coconuts to pay his bills. When he runs out, he goes home. So Pika works his schedule around him, except on Saturdays. Pika is ruthless on Saturdays. He's always here before Jefe."

"Interesting economics here," Lexi said.

She stopped and tilted her head, listening. Then she started swaying back and forth, snapping her fingers. Derek arched an eyebrow, and then he picked up on the bass rumbling from the truck with the iconic tune "Don't Worry, Be Happy."

He laughed. "I think that's Jefe's personal soundtrack." He lifted two fingers in a wave to the older gentleman swinging a machete. Jefe nodded and smiled in their direction.

"Maybe we all need to add that song to our soundtrack," Lexi said. "He looks like he doesn't have a care in the world. I bet his blood pressure is low."

Derek looked at Jefe again and saw him as Lexi did. He was focused, his blade coming down with precision on the coconuts. He was slower than Pika and Derek, but Derek had never seen him accidentally split a coconut open with a clumsy stroke. Jefe was a good father, too, and it probably wouldn't be too many years before his son would push the competition up another notch for Pika. Derek hoped he wasn't still depending on coconuts to pay his bills when that time came.

"Will you help me with this?" Lexi held up an expensive CamelBak water carrier. "My brother gave me this before I left. He heard there were a lot of great hikes here, and he made me promise to send him pictures."

"Sure." Derek showed her how to wear the pack comfortably. Lots of tourists on the island wore CamelBaks, but Derek had never had the money to buy one. His own backpack held a couple water bottles, mangoes, and granola bars—nothing fancy. "Let's get going. He won't believe it when you send him a shot from a thousand feet above the beach."

Lexi grabbed his arm. "Wait, I thought you said this hike was a piece of cake! Did you forget I'm from Chicago?" She pointed at her chest. "My heart hasn't been above a thousand feet for the past five years."

"Except on the airplane," Derek said. "You'll do fine. You look like you're in pretty good shape."

"Office treadmill," Lexi said. "Usually while Skypeing someone for an urgent meeting."

"Ouch. What did you do again?" He picked his way around the rocky beginning of the trail, which rose in a steep slant.

"My brother owns Burke Enterprises. He imports things from China and exports to other countries. Just think big business, lots of stress, minimum sixty-hour weeks, and you'll have the idea."

"So you must have got a pretty good severance package if your brother owns the company," Derek said. No wonder Lexi had some free time. Derek swallowed the memory of his mother working overtime and his own teenage years sucked away by minimum-wage jobs.

Lexi shrugged. "You could say that. I'm still figuring out what to do next."

"I'm looking for a street caller to sell my photos."

Lexi turned to him and smiled. "I'll be there. I haven't forgotten the mahi-mahi, you know."

"Pika keeps telling me that if I want to make real money, I need to take pictures of him and sell them."

Lexi giggled. "Well, he is good-looking."

Derek's heart dropped to the dirt. Of course she thought Pika was good-looking. Every woman thought Pika was good-looking.

Lexi casually brushed her hand through the air. "In a tree trunk sort of way."

A flicker of hope brought Derek's gaze off the ground. "Tree trunk?"

"You know, bulky but kind of a knot head." She grinned over her shoulder, letting him know she was teasing.

Derek laughed. "You know him better than I do. He doesn't know that I have some of him chopping coconuts. I took them when he was working hard, concentrating so that his body and face were determined lines. I think they show how some islanders live day to day and by the sweat of their brow. Some people like the pictures that go deeper than the surface. They like to see island life up close."

"I can see how that niche would be appealing. Do you do many like that?"

Derek lifted a shoulder and let it drop. "Here and there. It's tricky to get permission from someone, because then they think you need to pay them or give them free coconuts for life." He reached out as Lexi slipped, grabbing her hand. "Watch out for the tree branches. This incline is brutal, but we're almost to the vista."

"Remind me not to work out with you, okay?"

"It's uphill, downhill, flat, and more downhill on the way. But the way back always goes faster for some reason. Like I said, you'll do fine."

Lexi held his hand as he led her over another rock-encrusted part of the trail. He liked the way her slight fingers gripped his with strength. She was just a little thing, maybe five foot five and slight of build, but she held her own as they climbed.

When they reached the overlook, she flipped her braid over her shoulder and gasped. "I can't believe we're this high up. You weren't kidding." She leaned forward, still holding on to Derek. The turquoise waters stretched out to dark blue and then gray as they touched the horizon. The beach was relatively quiet this early in the morning, but at least a dozen people were setting up umbrellas and chairs along the shore.

It felt like they were a world away from Ke'e Beach, floating in a tropical paradise. The sun burst from the clouds, catching the golden highlights in Lexi's hair. He wanted to reach out and touch her braid, see if it was as sleek and smooth as it looked.

Lexi turned to him, appreciation in her eyes. "It's amazing."

Derek nodded. "And this is your first hike." He liked the open end to his sentence as they continued hiking, as if he'd said it was her first hike with him. He tore his eyes from Lexi and focused on the rocky trail, guiding her with him down the slope.

Chapter 8

$\mathcal{G}$oing downhill was much easier on Lexi's lungs than the uphill climb had been. She figured that if she went hiking once a week, in a few months she could keep pace with Derek without being winded.

"We made it." Derek pointed to the beach that suddenly appeared around a curve in the trail. "This is Hanakapi'ai Beach, or as Pika likes to call it, Stray Cat Island."

Lexi squinted, trying to figure out the meaning of Pika's name for the beach. She saw a beach surrounded with smooth black and dark gray rocks; several of them were piled high like little statues. Then she noticed cats lying on the sand, wandering through the brush, and lounging under a tree. "Cats on a beach? How'd they get here?" She looked back up at the mountain they'd just climbed over, and then back to view the trail as it disappeared up the next ridge.

"I don't know. Some of them are friendly, but most of them are feral." Derek walked slowly toward an orange cat lying in the sun and held out his hand. The cat stiffened, raised its pink nose in the air, and sniffed tentatively. Derek gently caressed the cat between the ears and down its back. Within a few seconds, the feline was purring like a motor.

Lexi stepped closer and held out her hand as well, letting the cat know she was safe. Derek took her fingers and placed them on the cat's back, smoothing over it with his own. "Are you a cat whisperer or something?" Lexi asked, and then she laughed at herself.

"Nah, I know Mango. He's been hanging out here freeloading ever since I first hiked this trail." Derek reached into his pocket and retrieved a baggie with pieces of bread and bacon. When he dumped it in front of the cat, Mango mewed and gobbled up the food.

"Did you give him that name?" Lexi asked.

Derek looked down at the ground. "I know it's dumb, but he likes it." He scratched around the cat's ears once more and straightened.

"I think it's cute that you have a friend on Stray Cat Beach."

"Two friends if I count you." Derek nudged her shoulder.

"Two then. That's a good number." Lexi ran her fingers through Mango's fur, hoping that the heat she felt inside wasn't showing on her cheeks.

"I brought a snack for us, too. You wanna sit on the beach for a few minutes?"

"That sounds nice. My legs are tired."

Derek led her across the rocky shore to the sand rippled by the waves. He sat down right at the edge of the waterline and kicked off his shoes so that the water creeping up the sand washed over his feet. Lexi followed him and wriggled her toes into the cool sand, enjoying the shivers sent up her spine. She unhooked the CamelBak, rolled her shoulders and leaned back onto her forearms. Derek offered her a granola bar and rubbed an apple on his shorts until the red surface gleamed. He took a bite and offered it to her. Lexi glanced at the fruit, a sense of intimacy swirling through her brain at the thought of touching something that had touched his lips. She took the apple and bit into the crisp flesh. As sweetness lingered on her tongue, it felt like they were definitely more than two strangers on a beach. Lexi found herself watching Derek's mouth, the way his neatly trimmed mustache accented the perfect divot in his upper lip.

"So, what do you think of your first Hawaiian hike?" Derek asked, as he reclined in the sand. His leg brushed hers and sent little zips of adrenaline through her body.

Lexi closed her eyes and turned her face to the sun, which played hide and seek with the clouds. "Mmm, I could get used to this."

"I think the island is slowly seducing you," Derek said. When Lexi turned to him with wide eyes, he chuckled. "Not like that. I can see the stress melting off you right here." He traced a finger across the back of her shoulders, and the movement felt like he'd struck a match across her heart. She leaned toward him, focused on that sexy scruff lining his jaw. Lexi swallowed and reached out to touch him. Derek's eyes flicked to her lips, and he smiled as her fingertips brushed his jawline.

"I feel different today." She studied his face, the flecks of green in his brown eyes.

"Me, too." Derek leaned forward, closing the distance between them to a breath that was charged with raw power.

A horrible screeching interrupted Lexi's almost kiss with Derek. "Ack! Charles, I chipped my nail!"

Derek pulled back, his brow furrowing at the middle-aged woman behind them. She traipsed through the sand toward them, her focus on her manicure.

"Sorry, dear." A heavyset man, most likely her husband, followed behind carrying a large tote with beach gear.

Derek looked at Lexi and rolled his eyes. He opened his mouth to say something when the woman started screeching again.

"Charles! This was the worst idea ever!" She stomped toward Lexi who scrambled to get out of her way. The woman stopped and held up her hand to examine each nail studded with glitter. Her fingers dripped with diamonds and gold. "I'll never get this sand out of my nails," she growled.

"Now, honey. The spa at the hotel can fix you up. Let's go." He took her hand, both of them oblivious of the romantic moment they'd just slaughtered. He led her toward the little paddleboat waiting to take them back to the catamaran idling on the ocean.

The woman continued muttering about her nails, her hair, and her designer clothes until the merciful roar of the ocean overtook her diatribe. Lexi looked after her and shook her head. "Wow."

"I wish rich people like that couldn't come to Kauai. They don't deserve it," Derek spat. "All this beauty wasted when there's so many who would appreciate it."

Lexi felt like she needed to say something in agreement, but she was surprised by the venom in his voice. She took a breath and said, "I never understood why some people take a vacation when all they really want to do is complain."

"If that woman gave half the money she spent on her nails to someone in need, the world would be a different place."

"Well, we don't really know. She might do that and more," Lexi said.

"No, someone like that doesn't give a red cent to anyone. She almost knocked you down while she was crying about her nails."

Lexi pursed her lips. Not all rich people were like that. She hated the idea that Derek would lump her in with that woman just because she had money. "It's sad. I guess all we can do is try to do better. I never want to become someone who doesn't appreciate the beauty around me."

"You're like a different continent than that rich witch." Derek folded his arms. "Money ruins people. She might have been a nice person once upon a time. Or maybe not."

Lexi forced a laugh and looked the other way, pretending to watch the ocean that suddenly looked angry as the waves pounded at the reef. Derek's accusatory words about money repeated in her mind, and her heart sank. It wasn't going to work. This dream, this idea of finding a part of herself she'd never been allowed to indulge in before would always be interrupted by the nickels and dimes of life. She'd tried to convince herself that she could have a normal life and enjoy all the benefits of being wealthy at the same time, but Derek's statement made it clear that hers was a false hope. She dug her toe through the sand.

"Hey, are you okay?" Derek's fingers grazed the side of her arm. "Talk about bad timing to break a nail."

Lexi couldn't ignore the way her heart leapt in her chest every time he touched her. Why did her money—or lack of money—have to be the deciding factor in every relationship? She pursed her lips together. "Oh, just feeling like life was trying to catch up to me for a minute there."

"Sorry, I tend to go off. Living in Hanapepe, I see the real island life, you know. There's a lot of people on this island who work really hard and deserve a chance."

Lexi nodded, not trusting herself to speak.

"Anything you want to talk about?"

"Probably not today. I don't want to ruin this memory. Thank you so much for showing me your world."

Derek smiled, but his eyes held concern. "That was only a tiny piece of my world. There's so much more I could show you."

They hiked back out from Hanakapi'ai, and although Derek pointed out several spectacular views and knew the names of the trees and some flowers, Lexi could only hear the angry roar of the ocean.

When they skidded down to the base of the trail, Derek took her hand. "Care for another coconut water on the house?" He smiled at her cautiously, as if trying to read her thoughts.

Derek was handsome, but the way he'd talked about rich people was ugly and hurtful. True, the couple on the beach was a ridiculous example of spoiled ignorance of the world, and Lexi tried to tell herself not to be offended. She wasn't like that woman, but Derek's generalized statement had blanketed her and Jordan and a few of their wealthy business associates whom Lexi revered. One man had befriended Jordan when he was first starting out and gave him valuable advice: "Don't ever take more than you need. Just because it's easy to make money doesn't mean it's yours to keep."

He lived by his words, and it was evident to Lexi and Jordan when they volunteered for his numerous foundations for refugees, illiterate children, single parents, and children of abuse. Burke Enterprises donated heavily to those foundations, and Lexi had even spearheaded their foundation for healthier living. Burke's Higher Steps taught low-income families how to improve their physical, emotional, and mental health so that they could have opportunities they wouldn't have if they were impeded by those issues. When Lexi thought of the hours and millions of dollars her brother had freely given to that foundation, her back straightened and she remembered her pastor quoting the scriptures. *Judge not, that ye be not judged.*

Lexi licked her lips. "Sure, I'm thirsty, but after that I've got to run."

"Yeah, me, too."

The coconut water didn't taste as sweet as the first time, but Lexi thanked Derek once more before she left. He held fingers to his ear like a phone, and she waved before turning to walk to her Jeep. On her drive home, she felt bad that she'd left so abruptly, but she didn't know what else to do. If Derek hated rich people, what would he do when he found out he'd been dating one?

Chapter 9

Derek chopped so hard Monday afternoon that he got blisters on both of his thumbs.

"Dude, slow down!" Pika hollered. "You don't have to kill the coconuts, just skin 'em."

Derek dropped his machete and massaged his hands, wincing where a blister had already burst.

"Come here and let Mama Kima take care of you." Pika's mother motioned to Derek.

He climbed down from the pickup and held out his palm.

Kima tsked as she rubbed her specialty ointment made from coconut oil and herbs into his skin. "Your hands show your heart. What's happening to Derek?" Kima tapped his chest.

"I don't know. I kind of lost my temper at some snobs up at Hanakapi'ai." He cursed himself for ruining the trust that Lexi was building in him. He was about to kiss her; they were a breath away. Instead he felt like he'd kissed his foot—or worse, Pika's.

Kima tsked again. "You boys." She patted Derek's hand. "Too much anger isn't good for the soul. Who decides who the

Great One loves the most?" She paused, and Derek felt the intensity of her question. "You?"

Derek's shoulder slumped. "No, we're all children of God."

Kima patted his cheek. "That's my boy. We've missed you at church. You come again, ya?"

"I'll think about it." He held up his hands. "Thanks for the ointment."

Derek brooded over what Kima said until Pika kicked him out of the truck and told him to "go take a picture of a turtle or something." The advice was good, but even the idea of a few extra hours with his camera didn't excite him the way Lexi had that morning.

Rich people had always rubbed him the wrong way. Growing up, there had never been enough money to do anything. He and his mom barely scraped by, and in high school, instead of hanging out with friends, playing sports, or even taking a photography class, Derek had worked as a cashier at the supermarket to help pay the rent that increased every year.

The rich kids had taken every opportunity to laugh at his thrift store clothes and scoff at him when he couldn't afford to take work off for the senior trip. Derek knew that he shouldn't project those old feelings of hurt and hatred onto others, but every experience he'd had with a rich person had been negative. When he'd first moved to the island, he'd taken a job at a hotel where he was bossed around by people just like that woman at Stray Cat Beach. It drove him nuts. They worried about their nails, their tan lines, and their tiny dogs, but they never noticed the real life going on around them.

He looked around the ramshackle home he lived in, a gift from his kupuna. It was seventy years old and a relic. For most of the past year, it had also been a money pit. Pika had moved in with him six months ago, and the rent paid to keep the lights on, but the patches on the roof weren't enough to last another rainy season.

Derek ran fingers through his hair and felt as if he were walking along the edge of Waimea Canyon. He had just a few months left to make his photography business successful enough to go full-time. If he didn't, he wouldn't be able to afford to invest any more in his business. With his house falling down around him, that meant getting a regular job, moving, and having to pay rent. He might be able to sell the land for a decent price, but the thought of selling a piece of his heritage burned the back of his throat. Derek determined again to change his future.

Could someone like Lexi ever be in his future? He didn't want to mess up a chance with her before they'd even learned more than the basic details about each other. There was so much left to say. Eventually, he did something that made his fingers shake. He sent a text to Lexi.

> **Hey, I'm really sorry about losing my cool on the beach. You're right. I don't know those people. I'm going to try to do better. I hope I didn't scare you off.**

Derek hit send and turned his hands over to inspect the blisters that had risen up angry and filled with tension, just like him. He gasped. There was only a faint outline of the blister; the liquid had receded and the burning had disappeared. With a little time, his hands would be smooth and whole again. He smiled. Mama Kima was right. His heart felt better, like there still might be a chance with Lexi. He'd just have to wait and see.

Chapter 10

Lexi was completely bummed out after the most romantic moment in the history of the Burkes was interrupted by a broken nail. The almost kiss was what she blamed her bad mood on, not Derek's outburst. His spiteful words had torn out the bridge spanning between them. It wasn't burned, and the timbers were still there, but Lexi didn't know if it was worth trying to rebuild the tenuous connection.

When Derek texted her with an apology, it sounded sincere. What grated was that he didn't understand why his words cut so deeply. She felt some guilt over that, because if she was transparent with him from the start, Derek would know that Lexi probably had more money than everyone on Ke'e Beach combined.

She groaned as she fell onto her bed, and the silky softness of the duvet cover brushed against her skin. A high-quality designer brand with a unique pattern of coral flowers on white with splashes of turquoise throughout the blanket cost six hundred dollars. Purchasing new bedclothes hadn't seemed excessive at the time, but when she thought of it from Derek's perspective, she felt greedy and stingy. She wasn't either, though. The one tie that remained to her work life was Burke's Higher Steps. She'd started the foundation, and while it was self-sufficient now, Lexi continued to help out. She loved to brainstorm new ideas to help more families and continue to spread the word of how a few small lifestyle changes *could* change someone's whole life. What would Derek think if he knew that Lexi had personally donated six million to start Higher Steps?

She shouldn't have to flaunt her charity expense record to win someone over. She wasn't her money. She was Lexi Burke, a thirty-two-year-old educated woman, a daughter who missed her parents every day, a sister who worried about her brother— she was just Lexi. She chewed on her bottom lip, mulling over how to answer Derek.

Whenever Lexi was stumped, she thought of her best friend, Gracie. She was a ray of sunshine, always full of life and reaching for ways to shower joy on others. Lexi checked the time to make sure it wouldn't be the middle of the night in New York. It was close, so she dialed quickly, hoping to catch Gracie before she turned in for the night.

"Lexi? Is this my Hawaiian sista?" Gracie squealed. "How are you?"

"Missing your happy voice, that's how," Lexi replied. "This radio silence I inflicted on myself has to end now."

"Goodness, I know. It was all I could do not to call you every day."

"I know. I'm glad I insisted, 'cause I talked to Jordy the other day and it's like he's on another planet now."

"Someday your good sense will rub off on that man of steel."

Lexi laughed. "So what are you up to?"

"Stretching before bed, you know the drill." Gracie's voice dropped a few notches.

Lexi could imagine Gracie, a ballerina of exquisite talent and ability, bent over with her forehead on her feet or lifting one foot above her head in a perfect split with pointed toes. Gracie was a little younger than Lexi, but she'd already been dancing on the professional stage at a grueling pace for over fifteen years.

"I saw the reviews for your last performance," Lexi ventured. "I'm sorry that one critic had bugs on his toast for breakfast." Gracie didn't laugh, and the absence of her giggle left Lexi speechless. "Gracie, are you okay?"

"No, I'm a wreck. I'm too old. I'm too tall. My feet are tired. I need to lose five more pounds. No one loves me." Gracie's complaints came out in quick bursts. "My agent told me that maybe it's time to explore something different, to end on a good note. There aren't many roles that I haven't already played, and the ones that are left are being filled by younger ballerinas."

"There's some truth to that, but what do you want to do?"

"I don't know. Maybe take some time off. Regroup."

"Gracie girl, you have to come visit me!" Lexi bounced up on her toes as she watched the ocean from her kitchen window.

"Now that would be a dream come true," Gracie replied.

"Then come. You can get away for a week to find your center."

"How will that help me decide what to do?"

"How long until the next audition?" Lexi asked.

"Four weeks. If I want to try for the lead, I'm already behind."

"You sound stressed. Where's my happy-dancing-feet friend?"

Gracie laughed, but it sounded hollow. She sniffed and cleared her throat. "I don't know."

"That's it. I'm booking you a flight. I have all the time in the world right now, and I'm going stir crazy. Come visit me. You can practice here just as easily as you can in Manhattan."

"Lexi, I'm falling apart," Gracie whispered. "Everything I've worked for my whole life . . . I don't know what to do."

Lexi flipped open her laptop and found a flight with a couple connections. Gracie could leave for Kauai in four days. "I have my finger hovering over the mouse. I really don't want to take no for an answer, so please say yes. I'll book you a flight. You'll be here Saturday."

She heard shuffling and another sniffle. "Okay, I'll pack my bags."

"Squeee!" Lexi cheered. She heard Gracie laugh. "I'm going to have you squealing by Sunday. I miss your enthusiasm."

"I'll be there. But hey, that isn't why you called, is it?"

Lexi had completely forgotten about Derek, but everything came rushing back as soon as she thought his name. "Well, there's this guy."

"Okay, I'm packing my bag right now. If Lexi the workaholic has been on a date already, then Kauai must be pure magic."

"Two dates," Lexi said softly.

"What? Are you kidding? That's great news!"

"I think it is, but I have a little dilemma," Lexi replied. "He doesn't know about my money."

"Hmm, I don't see the problem. Isn't that what you've always wanted?"

"Yes, but unfortunately his views of the wealthy are less than savory."

"Because he's a hard worker who's never caught a break, or because he's a bum who thinks he deserves everything?" Gracie demanded.

"He's a hard worker. You should see him chopping coconuts, and he's a photographer, too. I met him at the craft store and then at art night."

"Oh man, sounds like you've got it bad. So what's the big deal? He doesn't need to know the status of your bank account right now. For all you know, he could be a millionaire, too, right?"

Lexi thought about that for a moment. "It could work, but he was pretty vocal about some rich snobs we ran into on the beach today."

"Well, there's your answer. If you thought they were snobs, they probably were. Maybe he's never met a nice rich person."

Lexi heard movement in the background, a zipper being pulled. "Wait, are you really packing right now? Isn't it, like, almost midnight there?"

"Like I said, if Lexi Burke has been on two dates in one week, then I'm coming to make sure she hasn't been abducted by aliens."

"You didn't say that." Lexi scrolled through the screen of flights again. "Wait, there's a flight that leaves tomorrow night.

It has an extra layover, but you could be here by Wednesday. What do you think?"

"Holy cow! Weren't you just asking me why I was packing after midnight? I'll never be able to sleep now."

"Good. Less adjustment from the jet lag. Get packin', girl."

Gracie laughed, and Lexi smiled because she sounded happier. Lexi felt better, too. Maybe Kauai was magical, because she was already thinking of what she would text Derek and when she might see him next.

Chapter 11

$\mathcal{D}$erek pawed through a pile of dirty clothes near his bed until he found his phone lying under a pair of socks that should have been washed last week. Usually he was tidier, but his mind had been completely occupied with the new photos he was prepping for the coming art night and particularly Lexi Burke. Of course the battery was dead, so Derek had no choice but to start cleaning his twelve-hundred-square-foot home while it charged.

He'd just finished spraying down the bathroom when his phone pinged with an incoming text. The tiny sound made Derek's heart pound like it was ready to race right out of his chest. Two more pings chimed by the time he got to his phone. The first two were from Pika with the schedule for chopping coconuts, and the third was from Lexi. Derek's finger trembled as he swiped the screen to open her message.

**Hey, I can't wait to see you at art night so
you can congratulate me for winning the bet.**

Derek grinned and air-punched several times. It wasn't much, but it was something. He'd hoped for a chance to see her before Friday, but by the time he finished working with Pika and started prepping his photos, there weren't any daylight hours left. Kauai sort of shut down at night—at least, the activities he wanted to invite Lexi to closed with the sunset.

He considered whether he should ask her out anyway. They could hang out and watch a movie, though not in his pigsty. What if she changed her mind by Friday and decided she didn't want to waste any more time on him? Derek gripped his phone, struggling with the angel on one shoulder and the devil on the other. Finally, he texted her and asked if she'd like to grab dinner on Wednesday. Five agonizing minutes later, his phone dinged with her reply.

> **Would love to, but I can't. My best friend is coming to visit and I'm picking her up from the airport.**

Derek grunted and tried to think of a trendy, cool response that didn't sound like, *Man, I feel like a loser, but I wish I could see you.* He typed out ten responses before finally coming up with something half decent.

> **Sounds good. Hope you have fun, but not too much fun. See you Friday.**

After he hit send, he thought of five different things he could have said that might've sounded better, and then he decided to put his phone away and finish cleaning his house.

Friday seemed forever away, but Derek was taking Lexi's bet seriously. He did want to sell out of those turtle pictures and several others he was preparing so that he could take her on a real Hawaiian date. It would be nice to make enough money to take a day off and hike the Na Pali coastline for more fantastic photographs.

He wondered how it would feel to have Lexi photograph with him. Maybe she could hold his reflector, help him with his camera equipment. She'd said something about not knowing what she would do next after quitting her job in Chicago. Derek wished he had enough money to offer her a part-time job working with him. He scrubbed harder at his kitchen sink— that was a pipe dream. His heart was tangling up his head, trying to make him find a way to spend more time with Lexi. He didn't want to scare her away, so he'd have to be patient. He groaned and rinsed out the sink; at least the kitchen looked better.

A quick survey of his house reminded him of his humble circumstances. Lexi said she lived in Princeville, which was a far cry from the ghost town that was Hanapepe. He figured she must be renting something temporarily. Wherever it was, his little house would look like a shack compared to a Princeville address. But Lexi didn't seem like the type who would criticize the differences. He swept the antique hardwood floor and thought about how unassuming and natural Lexi was in any situation.

When he finished his chores, he grabbed his camera gear and headed to Poipu Beach. If the weather cooperated, the afternoon promised calm waters filled with marine life for him to photograph. Working would be the only thing to get his mind off this obsession with Lexi.

Before he waded into the water with his bulky camera, he tucked his thoughts of her away, determined to keep his head underwater until it cleared.

Chapter 12

*L*exi picked Gracie up from the airport on Wednesday afternoon and took her straight home, where the two friends reconnected on Lexi's secluded beach.

"This is fantastic," Gracie murmured, half asleep under a beach hat, her arms looking more golden by the minute. Her Italian heritage gave her the kind of skin Lexi could only dream of.

"I know. Crazy to think that I've been all over the world, but never made it to Kauai." Lexi sipped papaya juice and enjoyed the feeling of doing absolutely nothing.

"Ditto. I've danced in Europe, South America, and even Australia. I'm so glad you twisted my arm to get me here."

"Twisted your arm? More like caught you when you jumped."

Gracie adjusted her hat and sat up in the beach chair. "Have you talked to Derek today?"

Lexi shook her head. "Not since Monday. I've texted back and forth with him, but kept things sort of low-key."

"Dang, now I feel like I'm in the way. You should totally be out on the town with him right now."

Lexi swatted Gracie's arm. "Aren't you the one who told me it's a good thing to let a man marinate in his own desire?"

Gracie snorted. "Man, I must have been reading too many romance novels. But that *is* a good line."

"Yep, it is, but why do I wish that I had a picture of him right now to tide me over until Friday?"

"True. That is a problem, because I need to check this guy out. I thought you said he was a photographer. Didn't he take any pictures?"

"Not of himself," Lexi replied. "Remember the kissing sea turtles? I guess we'll both have to wait."

"I've never known you to be that forward, basically asking a guy out on a date," Gracie said. "Genius method, though, to disguise it as a bet."

"There's that." Lexi turned back to watch the ocean. There was no doubt that Derek was a hunk, but Gracie had a pretty good sense of people. If she thought something was off with Derek, she'd run the other way and drag Lexi along with her.

Lexi leaned back in her chair, thoughts swirling with Derek's thick eyebrows and contoured cheekbones. *Please pass the test, Derek Mitchell.*

On Thursday, the two friends explored more of the island of Kauai together. Gracie had a penchant for lighthouses, so they drove up to the Kilauea Lighthouse.

A short trail led to the lighthouse, and as the path curved with a great view of the ocean, Lexi stopped and pointed out a rock that was covered in splotches of white. Upon closer inspection, they discovered that the white things were actually birds.

"I love all of the surprises this island has to offer," Lexi said.

"You seem happy today," Gracie said as they continued up the path.

Lexi smiled. "I feel happy. Everything is so different here. It's like another world."

"Do you ever think you'll miss it? The office? The work?"

"Parts of it I do miss, but I think we miss a lot of our old habits, and that's what my former life was—a habit. It didn't bring me joy anymore."

Gracie paused, her lips twitching, and she frowned. "Maybe that's the stage I'm in. I wonder if I'm afraid to start a new habit."

"You've been working so hard for so long. Maybe you're like me, and you won't be able to realize how drained you are until you take some time off."

They reached the top, and both women laughed when they saw the tiny lighthouse that was no bigger than some of the quaint homes in the older part of Hanapepe. "I was thinking it would be bigger," Lexi whispered.

"I like it, though. It's another surprise. Maybe it's a sign," Gracie said.

"What kind of a sign?"

"I've been hiking trails, traveling all over, trying to reach the top . . . but maybe when I get there, it will feel like this." She pointed to the lighthouse. "I wish I knew for sure."

"I think that if you're not happy now, getting another lead part in a ballet won't change that for you."

Gracie pressed her lips together and looked out towards the water. "You're probably right. I just don't know who I'd be without ballet."

The mood was heavy, almost as if the conversation was drawing storm clouds from the distance. Lexi took Gracie's arm. "C'mon, let's go explore this lighthouse. You have plenty of time to figure it out. Maybe there'll be another sign."

"Does that mean Derek is your sign?" Gracie giggled.

Lexi laughed, but she didn't say anything. Her heart was too busy pounding out its reply at the thought of seeing Derek tomorrow.

Chapter 13

Lexi and Gracie arrived in Hanapepe about seven-thirty—Derek knew the moment she walked onto the street like a beacon calling to his heart. From across the way, he could see her sunlit hair under the booth lights. It fell across her back in soft waves tonight, and her dress flowed to her ankles. He thought about her hot-pink toenails and wondered if she'd switched colors. Man, he was really losing it if he was thinking about a chick's toenails. Lexi looked up at that moment and caught his eye. She started to wave, then looked at her hand and folded down her three middle fingers. Laughing, she flashed him the hang-ten sign. He waved back, and when she turned to her friend, he wiped his face to smooth out his goofy grin.

He had a few minutes to check his display before they came down the street to his booth. He noted that Lexi was guiding her friend along some of the other booths, probably taking her time while he sold a few more photos. Derek grinned. He hadn't quite lost the bet yet, but he'd never been so happy to lose before. The streets were busy tonight, and he'd already sold twenty-six photographs. The woven frames Kima had made were almost gone. That warmed his heart more than the excitement of money for himself. Finances were tight for Pika's family, too. If Derek could help Kima get away from selling coconuts for a few hours and rest her back, he would double his order of hand-woven frames and find a way to sell them.

Just before Lexi and her friend got to his booth, a couple purchased over a hundred dollars in photographs, including an enlarged version of the kissing sea turtles. Lexi beamed at him, and he didn't even try to tame his grin after the couple left and he tucked the money away.

"Aloha! I think you must be my good luck charm. I haven't sold this many photos at art night before."

"Really?" Lexi bounced up on her toes. "Does that mean I won?"

"I'll have to check the inventory first," Derek said.

"I should introduce you to my friend, Gracie Cardulo." Lexi motioned to the dark-haired woman with deep brown eyes beside her. "Gracie, this is Derek Mitchell."

Derek shook her hand, wishing he had a reason to grab Lexi's hand, also. But they stood on one side of the table and he on the other. "I hope you're having a nice visit. Kauai is the isle of wonders."

"Is that what they call it?" Gracie said, glancing at Lexi.

"No, that's what I call it," Derek said.

Lexi laughed, and Derek liked the way her energy seemed to flow through him, causing a spark that lit the embers of every thought he'd had of her over the past week. She studied him with a confident stance and that gorgeous smile. Derek wondered if she could feel the spark, too.

"These photos really are fantastic. Where's this one from? It's not here in Kauai, is it?" Gracie asked. The question jolted Derek back to the present, and he tore his eyes from Lexi to the stacks of photos in bins on the table. Gracie held out a panoramic view of Waimea Canyon.

"It is. That's Waimea Canyon on the west side of the island."

Gracie looked again, shaking her head. "No way, it looks like southern Utah. Well, this is much greener." She turned to Lexi. "I need to see this place."

Lexi nodded. "It's on my list of places to visit, so let's bump it up to the top."

Derek watched the exchange, wishing he could think of a clever way to offer himself as a tour guide. He didn't want to come across as desperate, but he desperately wanted to be with Lexi when she saw the canyon.

"Maybe we should ask the guy who took the picture for directions," Gracie said.

Lexi turned to him, and Derek's mouth went dry. Suddenly he was seventeen and tongue-tied. He swallowed. "You can go from the beach to this in about a half hour." He pointed at the picture Gracie held and took a leap. "I can show you where I took that picture."

"Tomorrow?" Gracie asked. Lexi nudged her friend, but Gracie ignored her.

"I'm chopping coconuts with Pika again, but if I get off early we could get there in time to take some shots and make it to the fish fry before the sun sets."

Lexi nodded. "That would be fun."

Gracie put a hand on her arm. "Wait, what about your date?" She pointed from Lexi to Derek. "Don't you owe her mahi-mahi? Or was it sushi?"

They all looked at the table, which displayed various sizes of pictures packaged in cellophane amidst the few framed photos he had left. It had been a very good night for sales, the kind of night that gave him hope and fueled his dreams. A buzz of adrenaline ran through Derek's fingers as he sorted through the photos. Then he caught sight of one of Kima's woven frames. His stomach dropped like a rock. Normally he wanted to win every bet he took, but losing this one had specific perks—like Kima's fish fry that he wanted to share with Lexi. He'd been looking forward to taking Lexi out, and now one photo was going to mess up his plans.

"There's one left." Derek slid a photo of the two sea turtles out from under an older picture. He tilted his head and tried to smile naturally.

"Wait a minute! You cheated," Gracie said. She took the image from Derek. "He hid it."

"No way. I always play fair," Derek said. "Look at my table. People have been pawing through these all night."

Lexi took the photo from Gracie, ignoring the lighthearted accusations between the two. She traced one of her slender fingers along the bumpy palm leaves and lifted her eyes to his. He was struck again by the vivid green color and hoped he'd have a chance to photograph her soon.

"Excuse me, sir?" Lexi held up the photo. "I'd like to purchase this illuminating piece on the story of true love. These two turtles seem to have it figured out."

"Wait, isn't that cheating too?" Gracie stage-whispered. Apparently Gracie's sense of fairness did not play favorites, and Derek liked her all the more for it.

Lexi elbowed her friend. The photo was an eight-by-ten and he'd marked it for forty-seven dollars because of the frame. "It's not cheating if I give it to you. Ma'am, I insist that you take this photo, because you are the only one tonight who truly recognized its beauty and meaning." Derek felt like he was walking along the edge of Waimea Canyon, holding his heart over the abyss.

Lexi shook her head and opened her purse. "I thank you, kind sir, but that would definitely be against the rules." She took out several bills and some change, counting out to forty-seven dollars.

"No, I can't accept that," Derek said, waving away her money.

Lexi grabbed his wrist. "Did I ever mention that I don't like losing? And if you don't let me buy this photo, you'll win." She grinned and dropped the money in his hand. "Oh, and here's a tip." She dropped an extra quarter in his palm and winked.

Derek shook his head, but Lexi pushed his hand back and lifted the frame up. "I really do love this shot."

He chewed on his bottom lip, debating between arguing more with the beautiful woman in front of him and celebrating that he'd be taking her out on a date very soon. He decided not to be a sore loser. Thoughts of Kima's fish fry had been roasting his brain all week. "There's a fish fry Saturday night near my friend Pika's house. I'd love to take you, and I hope you'll bring Gracie along."

"Oh, no. I don't want to intrude on your date. I can catch up on my reading," Gracie said.

Derek shook his head. "I insist that you come so that Pika will have someone to gawk at besides Lexi."

Both girls laughed, and Lexi's cheeks flushed with a dark pink that made the back of Derek's neck warm. Lexi tucked her photo into the canvas bag she carried. "I think that sounds wonderful. Would that be after the tour of Waimea Canyon?"

"Yes, at sunset." Luck was definitely on his side tonight. He'd come hoping to sell enough paintings to get a date with Lexi, and instead of just dinner, he'd be spending the entire afternoon and evening with her.

A cluster of shoppers headed toward Derek's booth, and he was torn between trying to sell more photos and continuing to flirt with Lexi. She noticed the people and adjusted the straps on her bag. "I wanted to show Gracie a few more shops. Call me tomorrow, okay?"

"I will." He lifted his hand in a wave. "It was nice meeting you, Gracie."

"Aloha," Gracie and Lexi said simultaneously as they turned to leave.

The two women had their heads bent towards each other as they walked away. Derek would've given an entire truck of chopped coconuts to hear what they were saying. Instead, he turned his attention to the tourists in front of him. After four out of the six people bought photographs, he wasn't sure if the night could get any better. He tucked more money away, excited about figuring out his profits later.

When he lifted his head, he caught sight of Lexi and Gracie across the street. As if she could feel his gaze, Lexi turned her head and paused mid-stride. The warmth of her smile brightened her eyes, and she lifted her hand, wiggling her fingers in a little wave. Derek flashed her the hang-ten sign and grinned. Maybe the night would just keep getting better.

Chapter 14

"Can we stop by that bookstore?" Gracie asked right after she caught Lexi waving at Derek. "I read about it on the flight over. They have a lot of used books, and I need more reading material."

Lexi refocused on her friend and commanded her heart to return to a normal cadence. "My Kindle is overloaded. I can lend you just about anything your heart desires. Have you read the new one by Lucy McConnell?"

"Which one? *The Reclusive Billionaire* or *The Protective Groom*? 'Cause I finished those the day they came out."

"You always were a bookworm," Lexi said. "Okay, we'd better check it out."

They walked down to the end of the street toward Talk Story. Lexi noticed the faded yellow paint on one of the shops and the houses down the street with broken shutters, sagging roofs, and peeling paint. She remembered what Derek had said about people in Hanapepe living the real island life. Derek lived a few blocks from this street. As soon as Derek stepped foot in her home, he would know she had money. Lexi frowned at yet another roadblock in their potential relationship, which would have to move slower than a sea turtle out of water.

"Now this looks like fun." Gracie stopped in front of the bookstore and studied the flyer taped to the window.

"What is it?"

"A masquerade benefit for refugees." Gracie tapped the flyer. "Look, they'll have Kauai's most eligible bachelors up for auction."

"It doesn't seem like something you'd see on Kauai—more like New York." Lexi scrunched her nose. "Still, it might be interesting to see who they bring in."

"It's not for another two weeks, so unfortunately I can't go shopping. But you could." Gracie waggled her eyebrows.

Lexi shook her head. "I don't think Derek will be up for auction." The information on the poster included a price tag of two hundred fifty dollars per ticket, so the event would only include those with enough money to make a difference in the relief effort. Lexi had been paying attention to the worldwide tally of refugees continually displaced and fleeing their homelands. She wanted to help. "It is a masquerade ball, though. If I was sure no one would recognize me later, I might chance it for that cause. An anonymous donation might be safer, though."

"So you're pretty into him, then?" Lexi asked. "I'd put him at eight-point-five on the hotness meter, and he seemed really nice, too."

"He's at least a nine. Didn't you notice his eyes?"

"Nope, not his eyes." Gracie giggled, and Lexi shook her head as they entered the bookstore.

They checked out some of the new titles on the front display table and then browsed the stacks of used books on shelves lining the walls. Lexi picked up a large book containing five different stories. The title, *Christmas Kisses*, caught her eye because she wondered what it would be like to spend her first Christmas in Kauai. How did Derek celebrate the holiday on this tropical island? Lexi smiled and hugged the book to her chest.

"Daydreaming about kissing Derek?" Gracie pointed to the novel and raised an eyebrow at Lexi. "Maybe I should play sick tomorrow. I don't want to ruin the possibilities."

"No way. Derek was serious about Pika. He's Hawaiian and very friendly. You need to at least rate him on the hotness scale before you think about bailing out. Besides, you were my friend before Derek. This is your time, too."

Gracie nodded. "Thanks, Lex. That's what I love about you. No one ever feels forgotten when they're with you."

Lexi thought about that while they browsed the shelves for the next fifteen minutes. There'd been many times over the past few years when she felt like she'd forgotten who she was. Remnants of Lexi Burke before her parents' death floated just out of reach, like a butterfly with silver wings darting between the clouds. If she could grab hold of that part of her, maybe she wouldn't feel lost anymore.

Each of the women purchased books, both new and old, and walked back out into the hubbub. A band down the street played Hawaiian music with ukuleles and steel drums. The light beat and cheerful timbre sounded almost like the ocean breeze playing with the vines of exotic flowers trailing from the trees. Lexi breathed in deeply, enjoying the tang of ocean, barbeque, flowers, and something else that reminded her of Derek. A magnetic force seemed to pull her toward him, as if every cell in her body craved his presence.

"Are we going to stop by and see Derek again?" Gracie asked playfully, noting the direction Lexi was walking.

Lexi scanned the area, noting the cluster of people around his booth. The Fuse logo swayed in the slight breeze, and the strand of lights above the nearby shop twinkled. "It looks like he's busy, and I don't want to be clingy."

"Hmm, you didn't seem pushy earlier," Gracie said. "If it weren't for me, I don't know if you'd even have a date tomorrow."

"I would've mentioned it. I just wanted to give him a chance."

"Wouldn't it be easier if you could just go up to him right now and say, *Hey, in case you didn't know, I really like you and I want to kiss your face.*"

Lexi pushed Gracie off the sidewalk playfully. She hurried toward her car with Gracie laughing behind her. Lexi shook her head. "Let's go before I change my mind."

On the drive home, Lexi thought about the masquerade ball and how she was already wearing a mask of secrets every time she saw Derek. Gracie helped her unload the car, and then they sat on the living room sofa, thumbing through their books and talking.

"So, have you decided what you want to do yet?" Lexi asked.

"About ballet?" Gracie pursed her lips. "I'm thinking, but I can tell that you're thinking pretty hard about how much that forty-seven dollars meant to Derek tonight." She glanced at Lexi. "That's like tissue paper to you."

Lexi chuckled. "You know that's not true. I've never been a spendthrift, but yeah." She ran her finger along the spine of her book. "I need to tell him before things get too complicated."

"Lex, isn't tomorrow your first official date?" Gracie asked.

"Officially, but to me it's a third date. Derek has treated me better than lots of guys I've dated over the past few years."

"And you're sure that you being a multimillionaire will be a deal-breaker for him?"

Lexi's shoulders slumped. "I don't know, but from what I've seen, my chances aren't good."

"Relax. If the timing seems right, spill. If not, keep those pretty little lips sealed. No use letting the cat out of the bag to roam the whole island."

Lexi had a distinct image of Mango the yellow tomcat roaming the rocky beach off the hiking trail. She smiled. "Okay, you have a point. Now let's talk about you."

Gracie leaned back on the couch. "Or we could just escape into one of these books."

"Have you ever wondered if our jobs became a sort of escape from facing the reality of life?"

Gracie looked up at the ceiling. "Hmm, I can see how that might elicit a healthy debate for some. But I've loved my job. Ballet hasn't really felt like a job until the last few years. I love performing, but it's not as fun as it used to be."

"It's interesting that you're facing the same dilemma as your best friend, right?"

"I thought of that on the flight over. You walked away from everything." Gracie sat up and massaged the back of her neck. "I don't know if I have that kind of courage."

Or money. Lexi bit back the words because they didn't sound right, but if she could say them, Gracie would know that Lexi didn't have as much courage as her friend. If it weren't for a seemingly unending bankroll, Lexi would've never left the security of her job. It brought Gracie's problem into a clearer perspective and offered a possible solution at the same time.

"All you have to do is a little visualization exercise," Lexi said. "Imagine that money is of no concern—it doesn't even exist. What would you do right now if money had no factoring in your decision?"

Gracie looked down at her feet. She pointed her toes and stretched her foot back. Lexi knew that Gracie was financially savvy and careful with her money. She was in a better position than most to take a leap of faith and change her life. Lexi also admired the strength that her friend did have to stop in her path and examine her life. Gracie licked her lips. "I've thought about taking some time off, but that's just a cowardly way of saying that maybe I'm ready to quit because everyone knows if a dancer leaves the stage, they aren't likely to find their way back."

"I don't know if you should call it quitting. You've worked for half your life. Maybe early retirement?"

One corner of Gracie's mouth turned up. "I'm just worried that if I walk away, I'll lose myself, my purpose. Who am I outside of pointe shoes?"

Lexi put her arm around Gracie and hugged her friend. "You're Gracie Cardulo, the most extraordinary friend a girl could ask for—in or out of toe shoes."

Gracie hugged her back. "Thanks." She sighed and leaned back against the couch again. "There's still time to decide."

They sat in a contented silence, and Lexi mulled over her thoughts—the ones that included Derek's handsome face. How much time did she have to decide whether the truth could be shared?

Chapter 15

Pika sold out of his first truckload of coconuts Saturday by noon, and Derek felt like Hiaka, the mountain god of Kauai, was smiling on him—until he saw Pika's cousin drive up with another load of coconuts. Derek groaned and rubbed his shoulders. The art night at Hanapepe had changed things for him. With a shot of confidence, he'd researched the galleries and gift shops on the surrounding islands and figured out how much money it would take to do some island hopping. If he could get his photos into more shops, he'd be that much closer to his end goal of working full-time as a photographer.

Derek looked at the pile of coconuts in the neighboring truck and turned to Pika. "Hey, bro, I'm ready to head out. Is your cousin going to help you chop?"

Pika pointed at the cash box under Kima's watchful eye. "You sure you want to miss out on the extra dough?"

"Remember that girl I was telling you about? I'm taking her and a friend to Waimea today. Then we're all coming to the fish fry tonight."

Pika narrowed his eyes. "You really think she's prettier than Lailani?"

Derek shrugged. "Guess you'll have to find out for yourself."

Pika chuckled and smacked him across the back, causing Derek to stumble among the debris in the back of the pickup. "Go on, then. That way when she sees me after looking at your ugly mug all day, she'll think she's really in paradise."

Derek rolled his eyes and hopped out of the pickup. "See you later, man." He hustled to his car while smiling at the tourists with a grin so broad they quickened their step to see what they were missing.

Derek was glad that Lexi had won the bet so he could take her out on an official date, and he was even happier that Pika's mom fried up the best mahi-mahi on the island. When Lexi made the bet, she was probably envisioning a heated plate with a sprig of parsley and a dainty side of rice that cost as much as three of his turtle pictures combined. Derek's stomach rumbled just thinking about Kima's special combination of spices, coconut, and fine bread crumbs coating the freshly caught fish. Not only would the meal cost a fraction of the price as an expensive restaurant, he'd have a chance to show Lexi another side of Kauai.

Derek texted Lexi to let her know he was off early from work. Since he was already in Princeville, he offered to pick the two friends up on his way down.

Taking Gracie to get some souvenirs. Can we meet you in Hanapepe at 2?

Mild disappointment accompanied the text because Derek was curious to see where Lexi lived, but he didn't press the issue. It was probably a good idea. He was sweaty and dirty from chopping all morning, and lunch and a shower were prerequisites to the beginning of his date with Lexi. He texted Lexi his address and wondered what she might think about the run-down shack he called home.

He pushed his doubts away and hurried home to tidy up his house and himself. Derek ended up scrubbing his home until almost two o'clock, which worked up more sweat to add to the layer he'd already accumulated that morning.

He'd barely finished his shower, dried off, and slipped on a pair of cargo shorts when he heard a knock at the door. He ran fingers through his wet hair, angled the top into his signature spike, and hurried to greet Lexi. She stood just outside his screen door with Gracie by her side.

"Afternoon." He swung the screen open. "Come in for a minute. I need to grab my gear and my wide lens."

"Okay." Lexi hesitated a moment before stepping inside. "This is a beautiful part of the island. It's so quiet—I bet you love it."

"I do. I'll be right back." Derek's heart thrummed as he headed to his bedroom to grab his camera. He hadn't seen a look of judgment in Lexi's eyes when she'd stepped inside his house. She was either a very good actor or genuinely appreciative of his way of life. He slung the bag over his shoulder and returned to the front room. "I'm ready now."

"For a bachelor pad, this is pretty nice," Gracie said.

"Thanks. This was my grandpa's house. He raised my mother here."

"I can tell it's filled with good memories," Lexi said.

"That and plenty of Pika's dirty clothes, but I try to keep those out of sight for guests."

The women laughed.

He grabbed the bag of dried coconut chunks he'd left sitting on the table and led them outside. Once there, he was confronted by his sad-looking Subaru Forester. The dent in the passenger door was streaked with rust spots, and the red tape over the broken taillight was a beacon of his financial status. But then he noticed Lexi's Jeep sporting its own rust spots and dents. He smiled. "I don't mind driving if you two don't mind my fancy car."

"I call shotgun!" Lexi scrambled toward the passenger side, leaving Gracie standing near the porch, rolling her eyes.

They settled in and headed up the winding road toward Waimea Canyon. Derek pointed out the change in scenery as the dirt and rocks became a deeper shade of red. When he pulled into the parking lot of the canyon, Lexi hopped out before he could get her door. She froze when she realized her mistake. "Oops! Sorry about that. I think it's been too long since I've been around a gentleman."

Derek smiled and offered her his hand. "Then let me show you how a lady should be treated."

Her cheeks colored, and he barely stopped himself from tucking a strand of her blond hair behind her ear. "I can't believe that this canyon is here. It seems like it doesn't fit." She held tight to Derek's hand, watching Gracie as she flitted toward the overlook.

"I came here a lot when I first moved back to Kauai for that reason." Derek swallowed. "I worried that I'd made a big mistake. Sometimes I still worry."

Lexi turned to him. "I think this is the right place for you. The first time I saw you, I figured you'd lived here all your life." She ducked her head as if she'd said more than she intended.

Derek tugged on her hand, leading her to the overlook. "That means a lot to me."

As they leaned over the edge of the rail, Lexi gasped in wonder. Derek smiled and took out his camera.

"This is amazing!" Gracie said. "How is it that I've never heard of this before?" She stretched out her arms and looked up at the sun. "I'm going to need a lot of pictures to remember this."

Derek focused his camera and pressed the rapid-fire setting. Gracie was beautiful with dark, wavy hair cascading down her back. Lexi had mentioned that she was a dancer, and he could see that in the long, slender lines of her body. He pressed the shutter button again as she turned to him and smiled. He appreciated her beauty, but he didn't see her the way he saw Lexi. Swiveling right, he captured Lexi as she took in the moment. Before she could move, he'd taken five shots.

"Both of you lean against the rail," he said. He hopped onto a bench behind them and focused in on the panoramic view spreading out past the two friends. Angling the camera, he caught the breadth of the canyon spread beyond them, with varying shades of red cascading down the deep gorge dotted by verdant green trees and shrubs. "Now Gracie, you move to the left and Lexi to the right. Look toward each other, then turn slightly to view the canyon." He motioned to them until they found the stance he was hoping for, and then he continued clicking.

Turning to the right again, he zoomed in on Lexi. She smiled, and he captured the color rising in her cheeks. Lexi was gorgeous. Her jade eyes stood out against the backdrop of bright blue and red behind her, her creamy skin and blond hair a striking contrast to the setting. This was the moment he'd been imagining since the first day they'd met. The contour of her cheekbones paralleling the exotic slant to her eyes held perfect symmetry. Derek knew these photos would be stunning, and a thrill zinged up his spine when Lexi turned to him and lifted her chin slightly, as if she knew he had forgotten about Waimea Canyon and was focused only on her.

He hopped down from the bench and crouched low to the ground, shooting upwards toward the brilliant sun lighting up the planes of Lexi's face. The gauzy white blouse she wore over a green tank top accented her eyes. She looked down and he closed the shutter on her dark lashes, nearly brushing her sculpted cheekbones. "Just one more, Lexi, if you don't mind."

She looked up. "I don't mind, but would you trust Gracie to take one of us?" The way her cheeks turned pink at the request shot tendrils of electricity through his arms.

He lowered the camera and motioned to Gracie. "You ever shot with a DSLR?"

"My dad has one, maybe not that fancy, but yeah." She approached Derek, but he moved the camera back into shooting position.

"Did Lexi tell you how we met?" he asked. "How she rescued that little girl?"

Lexi glanced at Gracie, smiled, and turned back to Derek. Her face softened as the memory hit them both. It was exactly what Derek had been hoping for. As her eyes fell into that faraway look of reminiscing, he clicked, moving slightly to capture ten, twenty, and nearly thirty photos. Pika came with him on a shoot once and made fun of him for taking so many pictures. "You're like a little boy playin' shoot-'em-up with the camera." Maybe the tease was warranted since he'd been taking pictures of flowers and lizards, but it took more strength than he would admit to lower the camera and hand it over to Gracie.

He gave her a few pointers and then went to stand next to Lexi. He tucked her close to his side. It was only a millisecond, but she turned to him, a look of appreciation and something more in her eyes. Then she smiled for the camera. Something was happening to Derek's heartbeat—erratic, uncontrolled, and yet totally in sync with Lexi's every move.

"Thanks for showing us the canyon. This is extraordinary," Lexi said.

Derek kept his arm around her shoulder and turned slightly. "I agree." He forced himself to look out at the vista, even though he wasn't talking about red canyons and lush landscapes.

Chapter 16

After they walked around the Waimea Canyon overlook and hiked around the red-stained dirt for another hour, Lexi followed Derek back to his car. This time, she waited for him to open her door. She noted that he opened Gracie's, too. Lexi caught Gracie's wink as Derek shut her door. Gracie seemed to be enjoying herself as the third wheel, and Lexi appreciated that her friend was willing to come along. It was probably a good thing, because the way Lexi's heart raced with every look from Derek made her want to tell him all of her secrets. Instead, she remembered Gracie's warning and Mango the orange cat. With a smile, Lexi tucked her secrets away for another day. Today was too beautiful to risk spoiling.

"The sunset from up here is pretty amazing, but it's great in Hanapepe, too, and we don't want to be late for the fish fry," Derek said.

Lexi nodded. "I can't get used to how early the sun sets in paradise." It wasn't even five o'clock, and the sky was already glowing as the clouds gathered near the horizon ready to enrobe the sun for the night.

"It's definitely a change that took me a while, but I enjoy getting up early now. The morning is when I do my best work." Derek rolled down his window as they coasted down the mountainside.

"There's something to be said about getting up before the world," Gracie added from the back seat.

"Maybe not as early as that, but Gracie is definitely the expert on mornings," Lexi said.

"How early?" Derek asked.

"Usually five o'clock, but that changes depending on my performance schedule."

"You know who else is an early riser?" He glanced at her in the mirror. "My friend Pika."

Lexi laughed. She couldn't picture the laid-back Hawaiian as a morning person.

Derek laughed with her. "I know, totally doesn't fit, right? Anyway, he loves to go deep-sea fishing, and you have to start early for that."

"Wow, that would be so cool!" Gracie said.

Derek glanced back at Gracie. "I'm sure he'd take you if you're here for a few days."

Gracie tilted her head to make eye contact with Lexi. "We're kind of living day to day so I don't know what our plans are, but I'll be here until Wednesday night."

"I'd better introduce you, then."

Lexi caught Gracie's eye, worried that she might not like the idea of the setup with Derek's friend, but she seemed excited. Maybe the change of scenery was helping Gracie more than Lexi understood.

Lexi put her hand out the window, letting the air caress her forearm. She kept thinking of how Derek had taken dozens of photos of her, and she wondered what he was thinking. When she turned to him, he looked back at the road as if he'd been staring at her. Lexi smiled and relaxed back in her seat. She wasn't worried about Derek trying to take advantage of her or having ulterior motives; the sweetness of innocence hung between them. There would be time to uncover the layers that made up Derek, and in time, she would share her own truths.

When they arrived at Pika's mother's house, the party looked like it had already begun. "Are we late?" Lexi asked.

"Wherever Pika is, there's a party. So the big guy must be here." Derek hopped out and helped the two friends from his car. He offered one arm to Lexi and the other to Gracie.

Lexi leaned forward and whispered, "Don't worry. There will be more guys than just Pika here. Just relax."

Gracie blew out a breath. "Okay. You remember the sign, Lex, right?"

Lexi snorted and then covered her mouth as they both started laughing.

Derek stopped and looked from one woman to the other. "Did I miss something?"

"No, but if Gracie starts braiding her hair, will you let me know?"

Derek arched an eyebrow. "Sure." He led them around the back of a house with a sagging porch and across the patches of grass and weeds that grew in place of a lawn.

They were greeted by about a dozen friends and neighbors. Derek made his way around the group, giving introductions.

When they reached Pika, Lexi watched Gracie out of the corner of her eye.

"Pika, this is Gracie Cardulo. She's Lexi's friend."

Gracie held out her hand, and Pika shook it softly, engulfing her slender fingers with his large hand. "Aloha ahiahi," he said.

"It's nice to meet you. I've heard a lot about you," Gracie said.

Pika narrowed his eyes at Derek. "Don't believe everything he says."

"Okay, but he told me that you don't look anything like a sea turtle, and I was about to agree."

Pika's dark skin flushed, and everyone burst out laughing. Lexi loved the lightness of the moment—Gracie was the only one who could get away with saying something like that to the Polynesian man, who probably weighed a hundred and fifty pounds more than her.

Gracie smiled at Pika. "I'm a ballerina from New York, and I'm here to learn about adventure. Derek said that you like to go deep-sea fishing. Will you tell me about it?"

"Fo' sure," Pika replied. "My boat is over here."

As they walked to the other side of the house, Lexi shook her head. "I don't know how she does it, but Gracie can make instant friends with anyone. I hope she doesn't break Pika's heart."

"It'd be good for him," Derek said. "He's been a heartbreaker for too long now, but I think he's slowly changing. It looks like the fish is about ready. You hungry?"

Lexi caught a whiff of the sweet and tangy barbeque aroma. "Fo' sure."

Derek laughed and guided her to the grill, where he served her a large helping of seared mahi-mahi. They sat around a fire on rickety lawn chairs and ate while the sun set. Pika and Gracie joined them, and Lexi waited for a sign that she was okay with the evening. Gracie nodded and smiled. Lexi breathed a sigh of relief. It wasn't like she was trying to set Gracie up with Pika, but it would be nice for her friend to have someone divert her attention from her rigorous ballet schedule.

"So, better day for coconuts today?" Derek said.

"I guess." Pika shrugged.

Lexi turned to Derek with eyebrows raised.

Derek put down his fork. "It's so weird. Jefe came early today and tried to take Pika's spot. And yesterday after I left, he undercut him by lowering his prices to four dollars. He *was* charging six." Derek scratched a mosquito bite on the back of his arm. "I would've been upset."

"I wonder if something happened to Jefe's family and he needs more money," Lexi mused.

"Yeah, bro. My makuahine said their water heater went out," Pika said. "His grandkids are living with them. Cold showers are no fun, right?" He shook his head. "I told him to show up early tomorrow. I'll take the day off."

Lexi caught a glimpse of Gracie's face, the soft smile of admiration toward Pika. His words cast him in a new light.

"That's good, bro." Derek reached out and fist-bumped Pika. "Wouldn't it be great to have enough to just loan someone money when they're in a tight spot like that?" Derek shook his head. "Sometimes this world doesn't make sense to me."

Lexi's throat clenched and she ducked her head before the flush of guilt showed up on her face. It was a perfect opening.

She could tell Derek that she had enough money to give Jefe a new water heater. She had enough money to buy him an entire house . . .

But she hesitated, watching Derek's emotions flicker across his face. He threw a stick into the fire, and she noticed how the flames hungrily licked at the dry wood, already working to consume it. Soon there would be nothing more than ash. Lexi stretched out her fingers, her mind running through scenarios where she confided her financial status to Derek. Unfortunately, every scenario left her with visions of smoke rising from her heart.

Maybe there was something she could do to help Jefe without Derek finding out. That's what Burke's Higher Steps was all about. She wanted to unobtrusively set up a chapter on Kauai. Jefe's experience was exactly what Derek had indicated when he talked about living the real island life. The fact was that poverty was everywhere; it lined every golden archway and rimmed the glittering diamonds in crowded cities.

Those plans continued to simmer, but the marketing side of her brain had already thought of a solution when she first saw the coconut trucks lined up at Ke'e Beach. She turned to Derek and touched his knee. "You know, I think you two could make a lot more money if you charged four dollars for each coconut water."

Derek nodded toward Pika. "He wants to charge five, but the competition is tough. There's a guy who sells his for that, so Pika plays around with his prices to sell more."

"But if you charged four dollars, I bet that most people would tell you to keep the change when they handed over a five-dollar bill, or a ten for two coconuts."

Derek ran his tongue over his teeth. "You really think so?"

"Don't some people give him a tip?"

"Here and there."

"That's an easy, built-in way to give him a tip that doesn't stretch the purse strings too much. You should try it next Saturday and see what happens."

"She's a smart one," Pika said. "Where you come from, haole?"

"Chicago. Worked in buildings higher than your mountain." Lexi raised her hand over her head, then let it drop to her lap.

Pika shook his head. "This mountain will never crumble." He looked at Derek, and Lexi wondered if they were talking about buildings or men. "C'mon. I'll show you my makuahine's plumeria tree."

Pika guided Gracie around the fire pit, his large hand spanning her tiny waist. She looked back at Lexi and smiled. Then she tripped over something in the darkness. Before Lexi had time to react, Pika had scooped up Gracie, holding her near his chest. She heard his voice rumbling as he asked her if she was okay; then Gracie's slender arm reached around his neck. Pika carried her into the darkness toward the crashing shore.

"See, I told you he was smooth," Derek said.

Lexi chuckled. "You, too."

"Nah, not me, but you—that idea would've landed flat in the fire if I'd been the one to bring it up to Pika. But he listened to you, and he'll probably make more money because of it. That's smooth." He interlaced his fingers with hers.

"What's a haole?"

"Used to mean a non-native person, but it's more for white people or tourists now. Sorry about the Hawaiian slang. He doesn't mean anything by it."

Lexi shrugged. "I wasn't offended, just curious."

"Just so you know, I don't think of you as haole. I think you're my golden girl," Derek murmured, pulling her closer.

The fire crackled and popped, sending dark orange sparks into the air that Lexi was sure matched the sparks flying between her and Derek. Laughter echoed around them, reminding her of all the people on the outskirts of the fire and under the patio lights.

Derek's eyes dropped to her mouth, and she could almost taste his kiss as he leaned toward her. He lifted his hand, cupping her cheek, his thumb tracing her jawline. "This has been an almost perfect day."

Lexi nodded, her insides screaming for the moment when his lips would caress hers.

Derek studied her face and leaned back slightly. "But I think we can top it. How about you?"

"Uh, yeah. Maybe?"

He looked over Lexi's shoulder. "Aloha, mama Kima. Don't worry, I'm behaving myself."

Lexi straightened and saw Pika's mother step out from the darkness and skirt around them, gathering up garbage and dishes. Her tsking sent Lexi right back to seventh grade when she'd watched her friends sneak behind the bleachers to steal kisses. She'd never been that adventurous, but right about now she wished for courage.

"She likes to keep everything on the up and up," Derek whispered. "Plus, she gets mad at me when I encourage Pika to hang out with someone besides the island girl she wants him to marry."

"Oh, that explains the look." Lexi leaned her head on his shoulder, grateful for his warmth as the night cooled around them.

Derek moved his arm around her shoulders and held her close. Lexi appreciated the respect that he'd shown to Pika's mother and to her. He really was a gentleman—and because of that, Lexi didn't mind waiting for a kiss that promised to be as spectacular as the paradise that surrounded her.

Chapter 17

There wasn't time for kissing over the next few days as Gracie and Lexi toured Kauai and spent time laughing like only best friends do. Derek had to work a lot of extra hours chopping coconuts and prepping photos for the next street fair, as well as helping Pika and Kima repair her leaky roof. The following Wednesday, Lexi helped Gracie check her luggage at Lihue Airport. "I wish you could stay longer," Lexi said as she hugged Gracie again. The airport was balmy, and fragrant perfume filled the air as if trying to coax travelers to stay on the island for one more day. The past week with her best friend had gone by too fast.

"Me, too, but at the same time I'm excited to get back and finish figuring out my life." Gracie tugged on her luggage strap.

"Sorry to complicate things by bringing Pika into the picture."

Gracie had gone deep-sea fishing with Pika all day Monday and returned with a sunburn and an inner glow that looked good on her. Derek had confided in Lexi that Pika was smitten with the Italian ballerina.

Gracie smiled wistfully. "I like Pika, and fishing was fun, but he has to figure out his life, too. I told him he has a big head and a big heart, and the only reason he liked me is because of my big mouth."

Lexi laughed. "You always speak the truth."

"I try. I just need to get the guts to speak it to myself."

"You already have it, but it's okay to be patient with yourself."

"Thanks, Lex, for everything. I'll come visit again."

"And once you figure out where you're headed, I'll come visit you."

"I hope things work out for you and Derek," Gracie said, brightening. "He has my stamp of approval."

"Thanks. He invited me to go on a photo shoot with him later this week."

"Meaning he's going to take, like, two hundred more pictures of you?"

"No, he's experimenting with catching the light at different angles on the water." Lexi noticed the signal that Gracie would be boarding soon. "I'd better let you get back to the mainland."

"My agent wants me to check out an opportunity in Chicago. Maybe I can catch Jordan while I'm there," Gracie said.

"I wish you could, and then you could bring him here."

"I'll do my best."

Lexi waved one last time at Gracie before turning to exit the airport. She stopped to admire the yellow plumeria leis hanging from a kiosk on her way out. Two women came up beside her and waited in line to purchase sparkling waters. They talked animatedly, and Lexi couldn't help but overhear their conversation. One woman had red curly hair that fell halfway down her back. Her friend's sleek black hair was styled in an angled bob. She was a full head taller than Lexi and the redhead.

"Oh, it's good to be back," the woman with the black hair said as she adjusted her carry-on bag.

"Isn't this one of yours?" The redheaded woman picked up a postcard, turned it over, and pointed. "It is! Eliza, you're famous."

The woman named Eliza smirked. "Yes, my photos are in the kiosk at a tiny airport. Let's hide from the paparazzi."

The redhead snorted and returned the postcard to the rotating display. Her phone dinged, and she studied it for a moment before gasping. She grabbed Eliza's arm. "JoNelle accepted Derek's application to the masquerade ball."

Lexi couldn't stop her head from snapping up when she heard Derek's name, but the women didn't seem to notice. It probably wasn't Derek Mitchell anyway. The two women moved to the register, and Lexi pretended to sort through a basket of tacky key chains as she eavesdropped.

Eliza drummed her fingertips together. "Oh goodie! This is going to be too much fun."

"Wait, what if Derek declines? After all, you're the one who sent it in."

"Everyone is allowed to nominate people. I just took it a step further to make sure he'd make the cut. And Derek will do it because of the cause. He's got that golden boy thing going on, remember?"

The redhead put a hand on her hip. "I still don't understand how putting him up for auction benefits you."

"Oh, you will." Eliza's voice was measured and cool. "Everyone will see. He should have agreed to work with me when he had the chance. Too late now."

The women laughed and walked away from the kiosk. Lexi moved over to where they had been browsing and turned the display of postcards around carefully. She pulled out a lovely scene of a pink-and-orange sunset and flipped it over. Lexi's stomach hardened. She wanted to believe that they weren't talking about *her* Derek. She studied the back of the postcard she'd seen the redhead hold up earlier. Crowe's Nest Photography was credited with the image. The logo was clever, with a crow standing in a nest of film strip. The initials E.C. were printed on the filmstrip at the crow's feet.

There was a bad taste in Lexi's mouth as she dropped the postcard back into the rack. The airport was eerily quiet in between flights, and Lexi was glad to be back in her Jeep. Part of her wished she hadn't overheard the conversation, but the other half of her was dialing Derek's number as soon as she started the engine. He didn't answer, and Lexi didn't want to leave a voice mail, so she hung up. She considered going to his house, but that would appear strange and dramatic considering the circumstances.

The more she thought about it, Lexi was glad that Derek hadn't answered the phone. He probably wouldn't care, but she didn't want to come across as paranoid or possessive. Derek hadn't mentioned anything about the masquerade ball, and Lexi figured if he was involved, he probably would've said something. The event was a week and half away. Hopefully that was enough time to do some research and find out if the Derek that Eliza and her friend had talked about was Derek Mitchell.

Chapter 18

Lexi's house seemed too quiet without Gracie. Everything was neat and tidy, so Lexi didn't have any reason to put off her inner artist. She rededicated herself to the painting she'd started the previous week. The scene looked different, more vibrant; the details of the palm leaves swaying in the breeze, the glittering sand, and the trailing flowers were all more noticeable today. Lexi recognized that the frantic pace of her business life was slowly leaving her soul, and she had a greater appreciation—and an artist's eye—for her surroundings. She painted the beach and the ocean waves kissing the sand, with a touch of the white on the crests as they rolled toward the shore.

It took Lexi several seconds to recognize that her phone was ringing—she'd been so immersed in her painting. When she found her phone, she was already sliding her finger across to answer it, too late to register that she didn't work with Shawn Halstrom anymore.

"Hello?" she said, noting that she sounded breathless. She forced herself to breathe, dropping her shoulders from where they had edged up near her ears.

"Lexi! Are you really there?"

"Yes, it's me. Is something wrong?"

"No, nothing's wrong," Shawn said. "I've been waiting, hoping that I've given you enough time, but Lex, I really miss you. Can we talk?"

Lexi leaned back against the balcony, her paintbrush clasped tightly. The cadence of Shawn's voice was familiar, bringing back memories of their time working together. They'd accomplished great things. If it hadn't been for Shawn's talents and organizational skills, Lexi might not have pursued the creation of Burke's Higher Steps. "I miss you, too, Shawn. How have you been?"

"Working too hard. Did you hear that I got a promotion to lead your foundation?"

"Really? That's great, Shawn. That was probably the hardest thing to leave. I'm so glad to hear that it's in good hands. You'll do amazing there."

"Yeah, I guess so. It's not the same without you, though." His voice dropped a notch. "I wish I could see you again."

Lexi closed her eyes. The waves rolled in slowly, rhythmically, with a dependability that would never be doubted. Shawn had been her rock, and they'd worked together with a rhythm that had kept their jobs and life in sync. She had missed Shawn, but not with the emotions she could hear in his voice. Before Derek, she might've entertained a future with Shawn . . . but the dark-haired man with a camera bag slung over his shoulder had changed everything.

"Are you still there?" Shawn interrupted her thoughts.

"I am, and that's the thing, Shawn. I'm really here. In Kauai."

"I know." Shawn sounded dejected. "I guess I just wanted to make sure that you're happy there, 'cause if you're not, I think you could be happy here."

"I'm sure it's hard to believe. It's like living in a dream, waking up here every morning, away from all of the stress. But it's a good dream. I'm living now, and life is beautiful. I never noticed before how simple things can bring such joy."

"I guess that explains why you added so much to the foundation funds," Shawn said. "Did you do that for me? For this job?"

"I wish I could take credit for that, because I want you to be happy. I don't want you to work so hard anymore, Shawn. Don't let life pass you by."

"There's someone else, isn't there?"

Lexi hesitated, and she knew the pause would answer her question better than any words. Shawn knew her too well. "I'm painting right now on my balcony overlooking the ocean."

"I didn't know you were artistic off the screen, but it makes total sense. You always had the best eye on the team."

"What don't you know about yourself because you work through every break, weekend, and vacation?"

Now it was Shawn's turn to hesitate.

Lexi knew she'd struck a chord. She cleared her throat and offered him the only thing she could: advice. "You still have time to change things, but you have to stop running so life can catch up with you."

"That's some good advice. Are you sure you aren't with Hallmark now?"

Lexi laughed. "Nope. The plumeria tree in my backyard smells way better than any cubicle."

Shawn chuckled. "I still miss you, but you've given me something to think about. As soon as I get an assistant, I'll take some time off and see if I can meet up with life."

"That sounds like a wonderful possibility."

"But Lex, until then, if you change your mind, will you call me? I'd hop a flight right now if it meant I could see your beautiful face again." He paused and cleared his throat. "I love you."

Lexi sucked in a breath. He'd said the magic words, but why now? Lexi curled her toes on the soft mat printed with Hawaiian flowers. What would she do if Shawn was standing in front of her saying the same words? Lexi shook her head. Even if Shawn was here, she wouldn't give up her chance to date Derek and discover what it was about him that made her heart soar higher than the mountains lining the shores.

After a couple beats of awkward silence in which Lexi tried to think of a response, Shawn cleared his throat. "You don't have to say anything. I just wanted you to know."

"Thanks. I'll let you know how things go around here, okay?" Lexi infused her voice with brightness that she didn't feel at the moment.

"Okay. I'll talk to you later."

"Good-bye."

Lexi hated the finality of the conversation once she hit the end button, but she didn't know what else to do. She'd never set out to break Shawn's heart, but he sounded as if she'd ripped his heart out and trampled it underfoot.

She sighed and put down her paintbrush. Shawn did sound different. She'd never seriously considered him before, but maybe her leaving had given him a dose of reality that could change his path in life. That was one thing to hope for.

Chapter 19

The next day, Derek took Lexi to the Shrimp Station so she could try *real* coconut shrimp. He'd offered to pick her up on his way back from chopping coconuts at Ke'e, but Lexi refused again, saying that she had some shopping to do and would meet him at his house. Derek had hesitated, and Lexi felt bad that he was probably wondering why she didn't want him to see where she lived. Her web of deceit was starting to tangle around her legs, dragging her underwater like a rope of seaweed firmly rooted at the bottom of the ocean. Lexi was ready to break free and tell Derek the truth, but she needed to find the right moment.

In between bites of crunchy coconut shrimp didn't seem like the right moment.

"Mmm, this is so good," Lexi said. "How's your day been?"

"Good, but something kind of weird happened today." Derek leaned his elbows on the table.

Lexi finished chewing an extra crunchy bite of shrimp. "What?"

"I got a phone call with an invitation to be one of the bachelors up for auction at the masquerade ball."

Lexi choked and started coughing. She grabbed her drink and took a sip, fanning her eyes.

"Are you okay?"

"I think a piece of coconut went down the wrong pipe." Lexi coughed a couple more times and sipped her drink. "Okay, sorry. Tell me about this auction." Lexi widened her eyes and smiled, but she was replaying the conversation she'd heard in the airport, trying to remember the woman's name.

"There's a masquerade ball that Kauai is hosting to raise funds for the refugees. They're asking local bachelors to participate and bring the spirit of giving to life on our island."

"That sounds like a wonderful idea. And how do they raise money?"

"By collecting donations, hosting an insanely expensive dinner and dance, and auctioning off eligible island men for a date. You know, the ultra-rich kind of party." Derek scrunched his nose. "I guess the event is good to get people to donate, but I took some photos last year. If you could have seen the costumes, the food, the decorations . . . if those people just stayed home and donated the money from all of that, we probably could have world peace."

Lexi laughed, but she thought it sounded a bit forced. "Even rich people need to have a little fun, though, don't you think?"

Derek took a bite of shrimp and chewed slowly. "I guess so."

"How many bachelors will they have?"

"I think there will be ten or fifteen." Derek swirled another piece of shrimp in the sauce. "They like the bidding to be just a step above friendly so that they can raise more money."

"Oh, I bet that will be exciting," Lexi said, trying to keep her voice even. She wished she'd been able to reach Derek yesterday right after she heard the conversation, because now she was worried. If Derek hadn't just bashed rich people again, she might have told him in between bites of shrimp, because then she could go to the masquerade ball and "buy" Derek.

"The nice thing about it is I'll get a little bit of free advertising for my business. They're letting me include my Fuse logo in the program, and I'll have a bio, too."

"That is a great opportunity. I wonder if you could get another venue in addition to art night somewhere on the island while people are still around after the ball."

"See, I can tell you must have been successful in your brother's business. Look how quickly you thought of that idea while I'm just wishing I had more shrimp."

"Well, have one of mine. I'm stuffed." Lexi pushed her basket toward him.

Derek smiled and snatched a small shrimp, popping it into his mouth. He bit down and some bits of coconut flaked off, one piece clinging to his chin.

"You have a little something there." Lexi pointed at her chin, and then giggled when Derek wiped his mouth, and the stubborn piece of coconut clung to his whiskers. She reached across the table, and gently wiped his face. The air between them was charged, and Lexi wondered how she'd gone from giggling at Derek to putting her hand on his cheek. Instead of pulling away, she enjoyed feeling the rough skin change to the brisk whiskers beneath her fingers. Derek covered her hand with his, moving his mouth and kissing her palm.

A thrill shot through Lexi. She wanted to be with Derek. She didn't want him to go on a date with another woman laced with diamonds and designer clothes.

The conversation at the airport slammed into her like a truck. Derek shouldn't go to the masquerade ball. Eliza Crowe was dangerous. That was her name. Lexi could clearly picture the logo on the back of the postcard. She dropped her hand from his face and broke the building tension when she met Derek's eyes. "Who is Eliza Crowe? I mean, do you know her?"

Derek's face pinched as if he'd tasted something sour. "She's a photographer. We met at a summit here on Kauai once. I thought it might be cool to date someone who had the same interests as me." He swallowed and flicked a pebble to the ground. "I thought wrong."

"Oh, that explains a lot."

"About what?" Derek turned to her.

"Well, I overheard a really strange conversation after I dropped Gracie off at the airport." Lexi repeated what she'd heard.

Derek raked his fingers through his hair and held his breath for a few seconds. He blew it out and shook his head. "I figured it was her, but I was hoping it wasn't."

"What made you think Eliza had something do with your nomination?"

"She's friends with JoNelle Walters who runs the masquerade ball."

"Wait, this same thing happens every year?"

Derek nodded. "JoNelle's been working on it for the past three years. This year is supposed to be big, really help some people; otherwise I wouldn't have agreed to participate."

"But aren't you worried about Eliza? She sounded so . . . sinister."

"That's because she is. She wanted us to team up, combine some aspects of our businesses, but I turned her down. She's been angry ever since and went to some lengths to try to sabotage my business opportunities. But that's been almost a year now. People around here know me now, so I don't think she's much of a threat. Besides, what could she really do to me? I'm a nobody."

"You're not a nobody, Derek. You have a lot of talent, and she can see that you're a threat. What if she's planning to ruin your business?"

"How could she possibly do that? Even if she did something to taint my image, it's not like people pay attention to the logos on their postcards and souvenir photos."

"That's true, but I've seen some nasty things in business. People can be ruthless. Ack! What if she tries to bid on you?"

"Don't worry. She won't be able to afford me, unless she has some kind of sponsor." He winked.

Lexi couldn't help but laugh. "Okay, I'll try not to worry."

But she did worry. After she left Derek to finish up the work he needed to do to prep for the following art night, Lexi drove home, her thoughts spiraling out of control toward a scenario where Eliza kidnapped Derek and took him away from her forever.

Chapter 20

Derek had endured Pika's teasing all afternoon yesterday about his new wahine, but Pika stopped when Derek asked him about Gracie.

"When you moving to the mainland to watch the ballerina?"

Pika shook his head. "I can't leave the island or my makuahine."

"You're right. Your mother needs you," Derek replied. "So you've thought about it, huh?" He'd been teasing, but the way Pika stared out toward the ocean spoke volumes about his feelings for Gracie. Derek cleared his throat, and Pika shrugged out of his trance.

"At least I'm thinking." Pika tapped his head. "You're a goner."

Derek laughed as he recalled the conversation. He didn't care how much Pika teased him, because today Derek was taking Lexi on a photo shoot. He'd be in his element, and he was excited to show her the results of his experiments on capturing light on the ocean water. Lexi had seemed genuinely interested—a lot of the women he'd dated in the past had faked interest, but their empty-headed questions exposed the truth.

He met Lexi early Thursday morning at Ha'ena State Park, and they walked along the shore to Derek's favorite entry spot to the Tunnels of Kauai. "Are you ready for this?" Derek asked as he snapped the waterproof case around his camera.

"Yep, I even practiced this morning." Lexi adjusted the rash guard that Derek had given her the first time they went snorkeling.

Seeing her in his shirt sent heat through his core, and he had to remind himself to concentrate on the ocean instead of the beautiful woman next to him. "Tunnels is like nothing you'll see anywhere else on the island." Derek pointed toward the reef in the distance. "They call it Tunnels because there are pathways through the rocks, filled with coral, deep caverns, and it reaches out to the reef."

"It's hard to imagine that so much is under the surface when I'm standing here in the sand," Lexi said, grinning. "I'm excited."

"Let's go, then. This will rock your world."

A few minutes later, Derek led her out past the first outcropping of rock, where the ocean dropped away from the shallow six-foot ledge below to a thirty-foot cavern. Lexi splashed in the water and grabbed on to his arm. She lifted her head out of the water.

"It's so deep!" She turned her head as if to check that they were only a couple hundred yards from the shore.

"Yeah, it blew my mind the first time, too," Derek said. "You okay? It just gets better from here. And don't worry, you'll float. Remember, it doesn't matter how deep the water is;

what matters is the current. We'll be swimming along with it toward Ha'ena."

Lexi nodded. "Stay close, okay?"

"I'll hold your hand until I'm ready to take some pictures." Derek's camera hung from his neck, waiting to capture another unique shot to add to his portfolio.

"Let's go." Lexi gave him a thumbs-up and then put her face in the water.

They swam along the surface, with Derek guiding Lexi around more outcroppings of rocks. They passed several schools of fish that were familiar to him. He'd taken plenty of shots of the bandtail goatfish, the Hawaiian cleaner wrasse, and the teardrop butterflyfish, yet he still admired their unique shades of yellow, green, and deep purple.

Lexi tugged on his arm and grabbed for his camera strap. She pulled him forward until he saw what she was pointing at: a school of bluestripe butterflyfish skirting around a bunch of dark pink coral. It was a perfect shot. He squeezed Lexi's hand and then let go to adjust his camera. Depressing the shutter button, he captured the fish as they whizzed through a hole in the rock to the other side. Derek followed, taking shot after shot of the fish sweeping in and out of the rocks studded with the jeweled coral.

Derek smiled and grabbed on to the edge of the rock, took a deep breath, and launched himself deeper into the water. He took a few more shots. As he rose to the surface, he bumped into the side of the rock ledge and cringed when his camera banged against the rock as well. There was a tug on his neck, and then the strap slid across his chest and floated in the water for a second. Derek reached out to grab the strap, shocked to see his camera sinking farther away. His fingers grazed it, but he missed. He blew out once to clear his tube and then sucked in a mouthful of air and pushed off the rock, diving as fast as his flippers could take him.

He kicked as hard as he could against the salt water pushing him back toward the surface gritting his teeth against the rising pressure on his ears as he fought to dive deeper. His camera was barely out of reach and sinking fast. A large school of fish darted around him, and he lost sight of the camera as he was propelled back toward the surface.

"No, no, no!" Derek dove back into the water; Lexi screamed when the water forced him upwards and his shoulder caught the edge of another rock. He gasped for breath and dove down again, but his efforts were futile. There were rocks and crevices everywhere. The tide would shift soon and his camera would move with it.

Lexi could hear herself breathing hard through the tube by her ear, but she couldn't calm down. She'd turned to see Derek's frantic movements and watched helplessly as his camera sank down into the darkness below them. She tried to swim after him and she'd been shocked at how quickly the pressure increased in her ears, and the powerful force of the ocean kept her floating near the surface. Now she understood the significance of diving weights.

She racked her brain, wishing she knew what to do, hating the anguished look she saw on Derek's face every time he came up for a breath. After probably twenty minutes of Derek's frantic dives, Lexi saw something that brought a surge of hope to her chest: a diver had just emerged from the water and was checking his gear a hundred yards from the beach.

She grabbed Derek's arm before he could go underwater again. "Wait, I think I see a diver. Don't kill yourself, just wait here, and I'll go ask him to dive for it." Derek started to shake his head, but Lexi tugged on his arm. "Derek, you can't dive down that far without equipment. It isn't safe, and you're going to pass out if you don't stop." It was strange telling him this, as if she were teaching him rather than the other way around.

He looked at the surface of the water, the torment apparent on every line of his face. Lexi didn't know what else to say, so she kicked with a burst of energy toward the shore. She swam up right next to the guy and popped to a standing position.

The Asian man jumped back. "You scared me." He was a head taller than Lexi and had short, straight black hair.

"Sorry, but I need your help. My friend is a photographer and his camera strap broke. He's right over there, but the camera fell down a ledge and we can't get to it. Please, do you have enough air left that you could help us search for a few minutes? I'll pay to fill your tank."

He furrowed his brow and turned to another diver floating in the water next to him. "We'll both come. It's not too deep right there."

"Oh, thank you. It looks really deep, though. Derek said forty feet. We'd appreciate it so much."

The diver next to him nodded and gave a thumbs-up. "Let's go. And don't worry about paying me. I'm here and ready; it's the least I can do." When he smiled, his features softened.

Lexi wanted to hug him even though he hadn't even started searching yet. Instead she swam ahead of him, leading him directly to Derek. They pointed out where the camera had come loose, falling so quickly through the water, bouncing off the rock, and disappearing from view.

The man, who introduced himself as Ono and his diving buddy Charles dove for the next thirty minutes until his tank was on empty. Lexi was certain every time they searched around another rock or crevice that one of them would come up with Derek's camera, but they didn't find it.

"I'm sorry," Charles said. "The current here is strange. It pushes and pulls against the tide and jets out sideways."

"Me and Charles are coming back out here tomorrow," Ono said. "I know it's not a very good chance, but we'll follow the current and maybe get lucky."

Derek shook hands with Ono and Charles. "Thank you. I'd like to repay you for your time."

Ono shook his head. "I'm retired and this is my hobby. I would've used up this air one way or another, so don't worry."

"Wow, that's really nice of you," Derek said. "Let me get you my info." His expression was pained, but he wasn't completely defeated yet. Lexi waded through the water to the beach, where he exchanged numbers with Ono.

"You two be careful," Ono said. "Tunnels is incredible, but beauty can be dangerous." His eyes flicked to Lexi and then back to Derek.

"We'll be careful," Lexi said. "Thanks again for your help."

Derek interlaced his fingers with Lexi's, and warmth radiated from his hand to her heart. The worst scenario she could imagine for a photographer had just occurred, yet Derek was aware of her.

They walked away from Ono and Charles and packed up their snorkeling gear. Lexi wasn't sure what to do. The despair hanging like a cloud over their heads threatened to rip open and drench them at any moment. Ono had offered a sliver of hope, but that's all it was—a tiny sliver.

"That man was really nice. He seemed pretty skilled, too. Maybe they'll be able to find your camera after all."

Derek wiped his mouth, which was tightened into a thin line. "I'm worried about all the rocks the camera bounced off. That case is durable, but it can crack. With the pressure, the current, everything . . . there's a chance that if they find it, it'd be ruined."

"I'm so sorry. Do you have a backup camera?"

Derek scuffed his foot through the sand. "I sold it so that I could afford a new lens."

Lexi tried to swallow, but her throat felt like it was clogged with the jagged rocks on the bottom of the ocean. There weren't any words that would help. She felt like Derek's camera, trapped between a rock and the pressure of the ocean pulsating with force that wouldn't allow her to open her mouth.

Derek slumped into the sand, his head falling to his knees. She watched as his composure cracked. They'd started the day with so much promise and happiness. Then everything had unraveled. His breath came in short gasps, his chest heaving up and down. Lexi knelt down beside him, holding her hand above his back, trying to decide whether to touch him or not. She curled her fingers inward, her own chest aching from holding her breath. One, two, three breaths in succession, and Lexi put her hand, light as a feather, on Derek's shoulder.

He looked up, and the despair in his eyes was like a punch to her gut. "I'm finished." His voice was eerily quiet next to the sounds of people along the beach and the rolling waves.

"I'm so sorry." Lexi's eyes filled with tears. She put her arm around his broad shoulder and scooted next to him on the sand.

"I don't even know what happened. That strap has never given me a problem. It has double locks."

Lexi's bottom lip trembled. It took every ounce of strength to keep her tears from falling. "It's my fault. I didn't mean to yank on the strap so hard earlier. I'm so sorry," she whispered.

He shook his head. "It wasn't your fault."

"But it was. I'm the one who saw those fish."

"And I'm the idiot who went in after them and then ran into the rock," Derek spat. "I'm the moron who just flushed my life down the drain. I just bought that lens six months ago!"

Lexi swallowed, but then she blurted out, "I'll buy you a new camera. This is just a blip. You can't give up, Derek. You have too much talent."

"That camera is worth six thousand dollars with that new lens. That's a car. You're not going to buy me anything."

Lexi flinched. She already knew his camera was worth a lot of money, but he was right. She couldn't buy him a new one. The stubborn defiance in his eyes was evidence enough that a purchase of that magnitude would destroy their relationship. Lexi sat back on the sand and leaned her head forward to rest on her knees. She'd waited too long to tell him about her money. Especially now that she'd heard about his poor treatment from the wealthy and disdain for rich people like her.

She swallowed the lump in her throat, and her mind cleared. There was a reason she was sitting on this beach right now—next to Derek. It would take courage, but she needed to act. Her heart swelled with love for Derek. She loved him enough to give him up if that's what it took to save his career. It was time to speak up and put things right. "Derek, I feel so bad . . . maybe I should go."

She lifted her head and turned to Derek. If she could say good-bye now, buying Derek a new camera wouldn't matter to their relationship. It would matter to him, though. He could continue his business, which was on the edge of becoming something great. Lexi closed her eyes and took a shuddering breath. With an exhale, she opened her eyes and looked out at the ocean. She dug her fingers into the sand and leaned forward, opening her mouth to say the hardest words.

Before she could speak, Derek turned to her, grabbing her by the shoulders and pulling her close. The tension in his chest radiated out from his fingertips that spanned her back. He held her close and Lexi put her arms around him, tightening the embrace.

"Lexi," he whispered. She leaned back, studying his face. His eyes were wet and he blinked rapidly. Her heart raced, and she could taste the salty sweetness of Derek's lips on hers. She couldn't leave him. She loved him, and now good-bye was the farthest thing from her mind.

"We'll think of something," Lexi said. She touched his cheek, moving her fingers across his jawline. She was tired of waiting to kiss him, tired of the interruptions. The whole mountain could fall on them, and it wasn't going to stop her from enjoying this moment of closeness with Derek. She leaned forward, closing her eyes as her lips brushed his tentatively.

Derek caressed her neck, gently drawing her closer, kissing her until all of her thoughts were captured up in a tornado of desire. He paused, and her eyes flickered open. She smiled and kissed him again, her hands resting on his shoulder. He deepened the kiss, breathless as he held her tighter.

He paused and whispered, "I still have you, and that's all that matters."

Lexi swallowed, and the tears she'd been holding back rolled down her cheeks. She nodded and embraced Derek again. She might not be able to buy Derek a camera, but she'd figure out a way to help him. The ocean crashed in the distance, but all Lexi heard was the beating of Derek's heart against her ear as he held her close to his chest.

"I'm not going anywhere," Lexi said. "We'll figure this out."

Chapter 21

Lexi didn't want to leave Derek alone, but she couldn't help him until she got home and made some phone calls. She dialed ten different numbers before she found the right assistant who could connect her immediately to Jordan.

"Lex, what's going on? You just interrupted a meeting."

"You're always in a meeting. This is your sister, remember? I know you were answering emails while pretending to pay attention to a PowerPoint presentation."

Jordan chuckled. "Okay, you got me there. What's up?"

"I need your help."

"Anything. Are you okay? You sound . . . different."

Lexi smiled. "I am different. You really need to come visit me."

"Wait a minute; you met someone, didn't you? A Hawaiian dude?"

"He is Hawaiian now, but he's not a native. He discovered a way of life that is amazing, and he's been working so hard. His name is Derek Mitchell, and he's a photographer. And he's solid, Jordy. I know you'd like him. He's so down to earth and just real."

"I can see you with a photographer." Jordan chuckled. "You always had a good eye, so I'm guessing he's good-looking."

Lexi blushed. "Total hotness, yes."

"So why do you need my help?"

"Derek doesn't know that I'm, well, really well off. He thinks I'm just a normal stressed-out business executive who escaped to the island."

"Well, that's true. You are normal, and you did escape."

"It goes a little deeper than that. He doesn't trust rich people or their motives, and I've pretty much created a disaster because I should've told him the truth before now."

"Why does he even need to know you're financial situation?"

"Up to this point, he hasn't needed to know, but he lost his camera in the ocean today. His camera that cost six thousand dollars."

"Ouch. Were you there?"

Lexi grimaced. "Yeah, we were sort of on a date." She told Jordan about the accident that morning.

"So buy him a new camera. You'll be his knight in shining armor, he loves you forever, and all that good stuff."

"Jordy, you don't understand. He'd hate me forever if he thought he was my charity case. I know I've made a mess; can you help me clean it up?"

"Sis, you know I'll do anything for you—or at least Porter will." Jordan laughed when he referenced one of his three personal assistants, who did everything from his laundry to buying gifts. "Are you sure this guy deserves you?"

"Yes. You said yourself that I'm different—in a good way—and you haven't even seen me," Lexi said. "I have Derek to thank for that. Anyway, what good is all the money in the world if I can't help someone that I love?"

"You love him, then. It's that whole L-word thing? Scary."

She almost laughed, but then she thought about what she'd just said. Part of her struggled with the realization that she could feel that strongly for Derek, but it felt right. "It is, but I can't stand back and watch him disintegrate. He's too talented. I figured you could help me come up with a way to get him a camera."

Lexi heard papers shuffling, and she knew she had Jordan's attention because he was taking notes. "Okay, so you need this done today, right?"

Lexi took a deep breath. "So you'll help me?"

"Yep, send me the deets and I'll put Porter on it. We'll figure out a way to get him a camera that doesn't look like it's being given to him."

"Thank you so much! I love you, Jordy!"

"NOW she loves me," Jordan murmured, with a chuckle in his voice. "Talk to you soon."

Lexi could barely contain herself after talking to Jordan. They didn't have a solution yet, but she'd seen Porter in action. She checked her watch and made a bet with herself that he'd be back with a viable plan within four hours.

Three hours and seventeen minutes later, Jordan called Lexi back with an idea that Porter had already typed up and sent to her personal email address. If Lexi could've chartered a helicopter without looking ostentatious and ruining her cover, she would have flown to Derek's. Instead she drove faster than was probably necessary, her heart pumping as she rounded the bend toward Hanapepe, unable to stand one more minute in a world where Derek was miserable and without hope. The sun was setting, and she wasn't even sure if Derek would be home, but she had to deliver the news in person.

When Derek answered the door, his face brightened before falling back into a deep frown. Lexi's heart was trying to beat outside her chest, and she wanted to shout the good news to him, but she waited until he motioned for her to come inside. His shoulders were slumped and his eyes were red and irritated. She wondered what he'd been doing since they'd parted, but she couldn't wait to change his mood.

"Derek, I have the best news!" Lexi squealed.

Derek led her inside. He brushed her lips with a kiss. "I'm listening, 'cause I think it'll be better than anything I've heard today."

She pecked his cheek and bounced up and down on her toes. "I called my brother and told him what happened this morning. Jordan just called and told me about a foundation for artists that his friend created. They're looking for ways to build the foundation as a tax deduction. They need a photographer who can take pictures of art in action."

"Gee, Lexi, that sounds awesome, except for one little detail." Derek lifted his hands to his face and pretended to click a camera.

"I know!" Lexi squealed again. "They're providing the camera! It's a Canon with all the equipment and a beginning budget of five thousand dollars to create the project."

Derek gaped. Lexi smiled and put her finger under his chin. She took a piece of paper out of her pocket and unfolded it.

"Here are the details. Read it over, fill it out, and send it in. I personally vouched for you, and Paul thinks you could be what they need to get this project off the ground."

"Would I have to leave the island? I mean, what kind of pictures are we talking about here?" Derek glanced at the paper and then tilted his head toward Lexi. "I want a new camera, but I don't want to sell my soul."

And that's why I love you, thought Lexi. Derek deserved this good thing to happen in his life. Lexi felt like she'd been filled with sparkling light as she thought about what Jordan had done for her. "Nope. It sounds like you would have creative control to produce the theme. And they're hoping for graphic design experience with logos and such. I wouldn't mind helping out in that arena. I have a pretty good eye."

Derek lifted his eyebrows. "So this could actually happen." He looked at the paper again, but his gaze traveled back to Lexi's face. "I can't even read. My mind is like Pop Rocks right now."

Lexi laughed. "Mine, too." She couldn't resist hugging Derek.

He lifted her off the ground and twirled her around. "You really are my golden girl." Derek let Lexi slide back down, her feet next to his. He cupped her face and kissed her gently. "Thanks for doing this. I know it was all you, and I'm grateful."

Lexi kissed him and then shook her head. "Not all me. My brother is a miracle worker. His contact list eats Rolodexes for breakfast."

Derek laughed and tilted his head, his mouth a breath away. His fingers laced through her hair as he leaned in for another kiss.

Chapter 22

erek thought about everything Lexi had thrown at him in the last five minutes. It didn't seem possible. A dream come true sounded trite compared to what she offered. He was desperate, but taking this job didn't seem like a desperate move. It seemed like the muse goddess had just dropped a bucket of golden inspiration into his lap.

He smoothed out the paper that Lexi had given him. The breeze from his window picked up the edges as he read. One glance over the contents confirmed what she'd explained. "It says they want to make a decision within forty-eight hours. Lexi, this is nuts. What if they don't pick me?"

"Then *they* would be nuts. With your portfolio, they'll be blown away."

"Wait, you've seen my portfolio?"

Lexi bit her lip and slid her foot along the linoleum floor. "Google is one of my best friends."

"Really? Amazon is mine," Derek said.

"Oh yeah, he's my BFF, totally." Lexi laughed.

Derek loved it when she laughed. Her eyes crinkled up and her pixie nose stood out next to her high cheekbones. Today he noticed a light smattering of freckles across her cheeks. She really was changing since she came to the island. "You know what this means, right?"

"That you might not have to chop coconuts every Saturday?"

Derek grinned. "That, and if they accept me, I'll have a camera in time to take shots at the masquerade ball."

Lexi's smiled faltered, which made Derek's smile widen. She was jealous. That didn't necessarily make him happy, but it did confirm that she felt something for him. Still, he didn't want Lexi to be uncomfortable. He was trying to come up with something clever to say when Lexi said, "I remember seeing a poster at the library now. I'd forgotten until you brought it up, but there was hinting of some celebrities coming to the island to bid."

Derek winked. "It's only one date."

"Oh, I—uh, I know," Lexi stammered.

Derek leaned forward and brushed her cheek with a feather-light kiss. "Good thing you're not up for auction or I'd have to mortgage my house."

Lexi giggled.

"No, I'm serious, Lex. I don't want anyone else to date you. It took one date for me to see that you're different. You make me want to be a better man."

Lexi sighed, and then she leaned forward and kissed Derek. Heat rose up the back of his neck as he held her, kissing her slowly and completely. In between kisses, Derek murmured, "I'd better get this filled out, and then we should celebrate."

"What do you have in mind?" Lexi's jade-colored eyes sparkled with energy.

Derek needed to fill out the form and get it sent in, but he didn't want to take his eyes off Lexi. She'd stepped out of his personal dreamland, and if he blinked for too long, she might disappear. He'd known her for two weeks, but they had a connection that was stronger than the year and a half he'd spent dating Carly. He pushed that thought from his mind and focused on the beautiful woman in front of him. "I want to take you to the Pu'u o Kila Lookout over the Na Pali coastline. It's my favorite place on this island."

Lexi stepped closer to him and put her hand on his chest. "Then I'm sure I'll love it. When can we go?"

"How about Saturday afternoon, once Pika runs out of coconuts?"

"Sounds good to me. But we need a celebration right now." She fished her keys out of her pocket and jangled them. "I'm going to the store to buy ice cream. Flavor?"

"Salted caramel and pecans."

Lexi arched an eyebrow. "Specific. A man who knows what he wants. I like it. Anything else?"

"Just you." Derek felt the heat from her gaze. Lexi licked her lips, and Derek thought it was a good thing she was leaving for ice cream so he could cool down, refocus, and not rush into things. There were big words on the tip of his tongue that he wanted to say to Lexi, but his good sense warned that it might be too soon. He took a breath and tapped the paper on the table. "I'll get this done before you come back."

"Take your time. I'll see you soon."

Lexi walked into the grocery store with a skip in her step. She kept seeing the look on Derek's face when he realized that he might be getting a new camera. The application was a formality, but only Lexi knew that. She was buying ice cream to give him time to send in the application. Otherwise she probably would've stayed at his house and kissed him.

She touched her lips. She'd been kissed before but not like that. Derek made her feel loved, cherished even, and she wanted to be wrapped up in his arms feeling the scruff on his face against her cheek as he held her.

Her plan had worked, and Derek looked happier than he'd ever been. How many times had the hard knocks of life pounded Derek into the pavement? Lexi wanted to give Derek a taste of a different life—one where he could work hard, but get lost in his art instead of stewing over how to pay his property taxes.

She tugged on the freezer door, where stacks of ice cream tantalized customers. Derek's opinions about rich people were like an iceberg—seemingly insurmountable, hard as ice, and possibly miles deep under the surface. She didn't know what it would take to overcome his prejudice, but she was willing to try.

On her way back from the store, Shawn called. She thought about not answering, but if he was calling to profess his love again, now was the time to let him know she and Derek were more than friends.

"Hi Shawn, how are you?"

"I'm good. I just talked to Jordan and he told me about your friend's camera. I think it's awesome that you're helping him out."

Lexi hesitated. "You do?"

"Yeah, here's the deal," Shawn said. "I know I sort of blindsided you when we talked last time, but I want to at least be your friend. I miss you and I miss us, but I'll take friendship over nothing."

"Thanks, Shawn. That means a lot." This was the Shawn she knew—he had some different goals, but at his core he was good, and he'd helped her through lots of tough times.

"I want you to be happy," Shawn said. "I hope we can stay in touch."

"You going through text withdrawal, too?" Lexi laughed. They used to text each other fifty times a day to keep up with all the appointments and deadlines.

"My phone is so sad and empty, you don't even know," Shawn replied.

"Well, I hope your phone can handle the adjustment. Tell it to slow down and take some breaks once in a while."

"I might just do that. Take care of yourself, Lex."

"Thanks, you too." She ended the call, appreciating how Shawn had re-established their friendship once he found out about Derek. Jordan must have known something about Shawn's feelings for her; otherwise he wouldn't have told him about Derek. Another point for her big brother, always looking out for her and trusting her to make good decisions.

She drove back to Derek's house with a smile. She thought about the masquerade ball and how easily Derek had read her mind. Were her thoughts that transparent? She'd thought up at least ten different scenarios of how to get Derek off the auction block without unveiling her filthy-rich status. The high-ticket dinner and ball was typical of a fundraising effort— pocket change for Lexi. The Eliza conversation left her feeling unsettled, and Lexi determined that if there was a way she could keep Derek out of Eliza's clutches, she would do it. It might take a pretty good costume to pull it off, though.

By the time Lexi arrived with her cloth bags filled with ice cream and goodies, the beginnings of a plan involving the very handsome face of Derek Mitchell circled in her mind.

Chapter 23

"I never see you so happy," Pika said. He tossed another coconut at Derek. "You look goofy."

Derek smiled wider and ducked to miss a piece of coconut husk that Pika tossed at him. He wasn't happy; he was overjoyed, elated, ecstatic, jumping-up-and-down-like-Lexi excited. After his most successful art night in Hanapepe yet, Derek had awoken to his phone ringing with a call from Jordan Burke's friend, Paul Reedley. Paul asked him if he was ready to begin working and ended the phone call by confirming the address they would ship the new camera and gear to.

Derek might've thought he'd died and gone to heaven, except that Lexi wasn't by his side—and he was still chopping coconuts. Her gorgeous smile and goodness made him keep his word to help Pika today, even though he wanted to take the entire day off and spend it learning more about Lexi. For all the time they'd spent together, Derek didn't know as much about her as she knew about him.

She didn't like to talk about her previous life in Chicago. Derek wasn't sure if there had been another man. She'd never mentioned anything except the brutal job she'd worked for too long. She didn't show up for his art night, and his disappointment had been hard to hide from the customers. When she texted an apology letting him know that she'd spent the evening helping Kima set up an online site for her woven goods and that time had run away from them, all Derek could think of was how much he wanted to kiss her.

A coconut husk smacked Derek in the arm. "Dude, you're losing your stride. Stop kissing that girl and get to work."

"Sorry, man." Derek chuckled; Pika had read his thoughts accurately. He chopped with renewed vigor. The sooner he finished this load of coconuts, the sooner he could kiss Lexi again.

Derek hurried home after work to shower and get ready for his date. Lexi would be there at three-thirty, and even though he tried to calm himself, his insides filled with anticipation. The lookout over the Na Pali coastline was a special place to him, and he was eager to see what Lexi thought of the rugged mountain.

When she arrived a few minutes late, she greeted Derek with a hug and a peck on the lips. She wore denim capris and a light blue T-shirt; her hair was pulled back in a ponytail. "You look beautiful."

"Thanks. You're not too shabby yourself," Lexi replied. "So how'd you get lucky enough to finish early on a Saturday? No competition from Jefe this morning?"

"It was weird. Jefe didn't show up until we were ready to leave." Derek stretched his arms over his head. "He said a water heater was delivered to his house this morning. Someone paid for everything, even the install."

Lexi smiled. "That's wonderful and good timing."

Derek nodded, studying Lexi. He wasn't sure why, but she didn't seem particularly surprised about Jefe's water heater.

Before he could ask, Lexi changed the subject. "So I looked into that masquerade ball, and you're right, there are some big people coming in. Did you know that the Christian rock band 7 Arrows is coming to perform?"

"They are?"

Lexi turned her head and smiled. "So you listen to Christian radio? You've heard of them?"

"Sure. They had that big hit a couple years ago that crossed over. It's the band with male and female singers, right?"

"Derek, you're going to hear them perform. I'm so jealous."

"I kind of think you're jealous of more than the band."

Lexi pushed his shoulder. "Hey, how would you feel if I was on the auction block?"

"I told you already. I'd mortgage my house." Derek was only half joking. He interlaced his fingers with hers and brought their hands to his lips. "You're my golden girl."

There was something behind her eyes. Her gaze had been soft, yet powerful. He shook his head. It didn't make sense, but when he looked at her, he saw determination, like she would do anything to be with him.

Lexi walked beside Derek along the path of red dirt, damp from the moisture that hung heavy in the air over Wai'ale'ale Crater. The back side of the Na Pali coastline butted up against the crater that hosted more rainstorms than anywhere else on the island.

"Are you warm enough?" Derek asked. "I can grab a jacket."

The sun was playing peek-a-boo with the clouds, so they alternated between the perfect temperature and a tad cooler than comfortable. Lexi stepped forward into a patch of sunlight. "I'm good now, but don't get the jacket. That's what snuggling is for."

Derek pulled her close to him, nuzzling her neck. "Good point."

"Thanks for bringing me here today. I've been looking forward to this since I saw your photos at the first art night."

"This is my favorite place on earth." He led her to stand on the edge of the precipice.

The valley expanded below them in a beauty that Lexi would never be able to describe but would love to capture on canvas. The ocean was a silver sheet sparkling against the skyline, and as they stood there, Lexi thought she could hear its distant roar, even though it must have been a couple miles away. Turning slowly, she took in the panorama of bright white waterfalls, dark green plants, and the ever-present red dirt in patches under clusters of bright yellow and fuchsia flowers.

They took pictures with their phones, but they couldn't capture the vibrant landscape in the same hues and varieties. They'd passed a few people on their way back down to the parking lot when they first arrived, but the area was quiet now.

Lexi's heart swelled with thanksgiving for the intricate beauties that God had created for His children. She was certain that she had stepped into a little piece of heaven as she stood in silence holding Derek's hand. A peace settled over her as the wind picked up, billowing out from the valley below. She hadn't figured everything out yet about her new life and her relationship with Derek, but it felt right.

Standing here in Kauai next to him was exactly where she was supposed to be. She closed her eyes and mouthed a silent plea that she could find the courage to tell Derek the truth about her past and how it would continue to affect her future. Back when she and Jordan were conquering the world, no one ever told her that being wealthy would be such a challenge. She wanted to live a normal life, but she also wanted to climb the mountains of the Na Pali coast and talk to God and then drive back down and buy a new water heater for someone like Jefe. She wanted to change lives, and because of her money, she could.

Lexi swallowed and opened her eyes. She turned to Derek. "I think I understand why this place is your favorite."

Derek nodded. The sun was sinking toward the water, promising a spectacular show of colors as it set.

"Will you bring me back here when you get your new camera? I'd love to give Jordan a glimpse of what he's missing."

"I will, on one condition."

"Okay?"

"That when he comes to visit you, he won't try to steal you away from here."

Lexi laughed. "I thought it was going to be something hard. Once Jordan sees this paradise, he'll stop asking me to come back to work. Besides, I can't think of anything that would make me ever want to leave this place."

Derek smiled and wrapped her in a tight embrace. "Me, too."

He kissed her gently, again and again. Heat rose in her belly, and she trailed her fingers along the back of his neck, trying to get closer. They missed the sunset, but when Derek whispered in her ear, Lexi felt like the sun's rays had collected in her heart. She touched Derek's cheek, sliding her fingers over his beard and tracing his sideburns. "You make me feel like I've finally come home."

He hugged her and kissed her forehead. "You have."

Chapter 24

Gracie called Lexi the next day to tell her that she had set up a time to visit Jordan when she went to Chicago in three weeks. When Lexi told her friend about the masquerade ball, Gracie wasn't surprised that Derek would be in the lineup. "He's talented and has more than just good looks. I'm sure they were looking for men like that for the auction."

"But I'm really worried," Lexi said. She recounted the conversation that had haunted her for days. "I told him about Eliza, but Derek doesn't really think it's a problem." She pulled off a few dead leaves from the violet she was trying to nurture in her kitchen window. "He said maybe she has a sponsor and she'll bid on him and try to embarrass him or something."

"You'll have to curl your hair. Tons of curls, pinned up all over."

"What?"

"And your costume will be absolutely stunning. Maybe in a dark purple. You look good in that color."

"What are you talking about?"

"Lexi, you're going to that masquerade ball. There's a reason you met Derek—maybe it's a bigger reason than you falling in love with him."

Lexi swallowed. She hadn't confessed her feelings to Gracie, but she didn't object to the conclusion that she'd fallen in love with Derek. "I can't go to the ball. The tickets are, like, two fifty apiece. That's a pretty big giveaway that I have money."

"Ugh, you're still not over that? Girl, you have one week left. Either Derek finds out that you like to swim in money in your spare time, or he doesn't. I don't care what he knows or not; you're going to that ball, and you're going to be the highest bidder."

Lexi bit her lip, and a tremor passed through her shoulders. She wanted to do exactly what Gracie proposed. Eliza Crowe was up to something, and Lexi had never liked crows anyway. "I don't know what kind of mask to get."

"Yes!" Gracie squealed. "Isn't it nice that you're a millionaire and money is no object? Because I just Googled masquerade ball costumes, and you are going to die when I send you this link."

Gracie was right. Lexi did about die when she clicked the link and it opened to a fabulous gown with alternating shades of purple with a golden sheer layer over the large ruffled skirt. The mask that went with the costume had a beautiful plume of feathers in white, gold, and purple, with golden combs that kept it in place. She closed her eyes and imagined Derek's face when he saw her in the costume. For a moment, she could see the appreciation in his eyes . . . but then they melted to hurt and betrayal as realization flooded his vision. Lexi shook her head. Maybe it wouldn't happen that way. If she could tell him before the ball . . .

But then Lexi remembered Derek's new camera that was on its way courtesy of her meddling, and her shoulders slumped. "There's no way I can tell him. I'm in too deep. I'll go and find out who this Eliza chick is working with. If she is the highest bidder, I'll beat her. Maybe I can keep my identity a secret."

"Lex, I'm worried that you're right. You shouldn't have waited so long to tell Derek the truth."

"I know. I'll figure it out, though."

"You will," Gracie said. "You always do. Now let's get your costume ordered. You're going to have to pay some serious rush fees to get it to Kauai in time."

Lexi enlarged the image of the costume, scowling at the photo and the trouble she'd gotten herself into. But then she clicked on a 3D image of the mask, and a smile tugged at the corners of her mouth. She thought of Derek's kisses and the way he held her like a treasure. Maybe after she surprised him, Derek would surprise her.

Chapter 25

Lexi spent every spare minute with Derek for the next week. She went with him to be fitted for a specially tailored sport coat. The light gray color brought out the green flecks in his brown eyes. Underneath, he wore a sleek dress shirt in hunter green. The buttons and lining were dark purple, and Lexi smiled when she thought of how he'd look next to her colorful costume. She helped him pick out a clever mask that went well with his beard. He balked at the one-hundred-seventy-five-dollar price tag, but since the mask was made by islanders and paid for by the charity organization, Lexi was able to convince him to order it.

She straightened the lapels of his sport coat, her fingers tracing the unique stitching around the edges of the fabric. "You look good."

Derek leaned forward and brushed a light kiss on her lips. "Thanks, but this isn't really my kind of getup."

Lexi touched the ivory buttons on his sleeve. "It suits you, though. You might think about adding a picture of this—" She motioned to Derek. "—to your portfolio and bio."

"For you, I might consider it, but only because you're some kind of business genius." Derek tapped the end of her nose.

Lexi admired how his broad shoulders filled the cut of the jacket just right. He'd trimmed his beard and hair the day before, and everything about him was crisp and desirable. A little thrill fluttered inside when she thought of her own costume lying on the bed in her spare room. She hoped that circumstances would prevent Derek from finding out her identity, but at the same time, she thought a picture of the two of them together could easily make one of the covers of the magazines covering the event.

"Lex, are you sure you can't come with me?" Derek asked. The way he used her nickname made her want to kiss him, so she did.

"To the ball? I thought the tickets were sold out."

"They are, but maybe you could help me get ready. And what about Oahu?" His voice trailed off, a look of insecurity passing over him. Lexi fell one more step in love with him. He was so humble, he really had no idea what his furrowed brows did to her.

Derek had been invited to hop over to Oahu on Thursday and Friday to participate in a publicity shoot for some of the big names coming in to Kauai on Saturday. With his new gear, he was like a kid on Christmas. Lexi couldn't be happier for him, but she would miss him.

"I want to come, but I promised Jordan that I would cover for him this weekend. I'm hoping that he won't end up needing me, but just in case, I'd better stay here." She didn't elaborate that the work she would be doing was for Burke's Higher

Steps—something she'd volunteered for before ever moving to Kauai.

"I'll miss you."

"But I'll see you sometime Sunday, right?"

Derek nodded. "Wish me luck. I'll call you soon."

With the help of Jordan's assistant, Porter, Burke Enterprises was registered for the masquerade ball, and Lexi had the authority to bid for one of the bachelors. A beautifully designed brochure was emailed to her with full-color photos of the fifteen bachelors. Even if Lexi wasn't completely biased, Derek stood out from the others. With his rugged, sexy appeal and the way his dark eyebrows arched over his deep-set eyes, Lexi knew there would be several bidders. She touched her computer screen where Derek held on to his suit jacket, the tendons in his hands standing out. She imagined the feel of his muscular arms around her and smiled. Derek was irresistible in more ways than his looks. With the help of positive affirmation, Lexi envisioned Derek's face creasing in his characteristic grin when she won the bid for an exclusive date with him. The outing would include a photo shoot where Derek would show the lucky winner how he worked and some of his favorite places on the island to photograph, including his undersea expertise.

Each bachelor offered a specific appeal for his exclusive date, and they included a range of talents. There was a helicopter pilot from one of the local tour companies, a captain of a deep-sea fishing vessel, an actor, an agronomist from the farming sector of Kauai's lush fields, a novelist, and a prize-winning surfer.

There were dozens of sponsors for the event, and if she could keep Derek safe from Eliza, Burke Enterprises would be a regular contributor so that he wouldn't ever have to be up for auction again.

On the day of the masquerade ball, Lexi's nerves were frayed. She'd spent several hours trolling the internet and studying Eliza Crowe, but hadn't discovered her motive. Lexi even enlisted the help of one of her old virtual assistants, and finally, on Saturday morning, they found a suspicious-looking tweet.

The message trail indicated that Eliza had been positioning herself to get in the good graces of a large souvenir photography company called GlobePhoto. Lexi studied the short sentence, scrutinizing it for any hidden meaning she was missing.

My new partner & I will be swapping photos tomorrow pre-masquerade ball to prep for our debut with GlobePhoto! Aloha world!

Lexi tried to tell herself that it didn't have anything to do with Derek, but every time she read it, chills ran along the back of her shoulders. Derek was a prime candidate for a company like GlobePhoto because of his experience capturing the different terrains of Kauai. But Derek would never agree to give up his own company to go with the huge conglomerate, especially now that he was involved with his new venture. Lexi and her personal assistant searched through every piece of information they could find, but there were no clues as to how Eliza might be able to pressure Derek into working with her.

Trying to get her mind to rest, Lexi clicked back to the image of Derek in his new jacket. Man, he was good-looking. Reading over the summary of his date made something click in her mind that filled her stomach with ice. The winning date for Derek included taking the person on a photo shoot to watch him work, specifically his unique underwater photography. He was one of the few on the island who could capture marine life in a way that sparked the interest of everyone from casual admirers to other photographers. Was Eliza hoping to steal his techniques, or would she form an alliance with GlobePhoto behind Derek's back?

Lexi shook her head. It didn't matter if she couldn't solve the mystery, as long as she kept Derek out of Eliza's clutches.

Chapter 26

Derek craned his neck, trying to follow the woman in the purple dress. Her blond curls were pinned up loosely around her feathered mask, which covered more of her face than some of the other masks he'd seen. The way she moved reminded him of Lexi. From across the room he'd been certain it was her, but Lexi always wore her hair straight.

In his hurry to follow her, he almost ran into Eliza Crowe, who gave him an appraising look. "Well, good evening, Derek. Are you enjoying yourself?"

"I am. It looks like the night will be a success."

"Oh, this is just the beginning." Eliza ran her fingers down Derek's forearm. She wore black gloves that reached past her elbows. "There are some huge sponsors here, and I happen to know that one of them is interested in you."

Derek pretended not to be concerned, but he was starting to worry. What if JoNelle was helping front a bid for Eliza? He recalled Lexi's warnings about his overzealous competition. For the first time, he wished he'd taken her advice and found a sponsor.

Eliza scrutinized him, waiting for an answer. "You have a lot of talent, and people are starting to take notice," she purred.

"Thank you. I enjoy my work—for me, it requires solitude to get into the zone. I'm just grateful that my photography can do something positive for Kauai and the local economy." He tightened his jaw because he sounded like a dork, but he hoped Eliza caught the hint. She narrowed her eyes, and Derek remembered how hard she'd tried to convince him to form a partnership with her when he first came to Kauai.

"You'd be wise to consider all of your options." Eliza placed a hand on her chest, as if he should consider her as one of his options.

"I told you before that I'm not interested in working with you, regardless of the circumstances." Derek's words were flat.

Eliza shrugged and took a step away from him, but then she turned her head and called over her shoulder, "Oh, did you hear? They're changing up the booth spaces at art night. I doubt Hanapepe will be seeing much more of Fuse Photography."

Derek swiveled on his heel without a reply. How could Eliza mess with his space at art night? He strode across the room toward the stage, looking for JoNelle. He needed to do something to keep Eliza from bidding on him. Lexi had been right—whatever Eliza had planned, it wasn't good.

He scanned the room, but when he found JoNelle she was holding a microphone. "Ladies and gentlemen, it's time for the auction to begin. The bachelors are on their way to the stage now. Please prepare yourselves for this exciting event."

Derek's steps were robotic as he moved toward the stage. JoNelle's announcement faded behind the ringing in his ears.

He tried to reassure himself that Eliza couldn't hurt him, but the fact that she knew about his booth at art night was not a good sign.

As he climbed the steps to the stage and turned to face the crowd, looking for Eliza, his eyes landed on the blond woman in the beautiful purple-and-gold dress he'd seen before. She was watching him, but she ducked behind someone else when he caught her eye.

Derek took a deep breath. *Lexi's not here,* he thought, *but I wish she was.*

Lexi had barely escaped when Derek spotted her. It thrilled her that his gaze had turned to one of recognition and curiosity, but at the same time, she panicked as she hurried through the ball gowns, trying not to trip in her six-inch heels. The masquerade ball was glorious, with Hawaiian greenery, plumeria, bougainvillea, and palm trees dotting the room. White twinkle lights were draped around the entryways, and the stage looked like it was a cross between a medieval castle and a Hawaiian paradise. But Lexi wasn't concentrating on the décor or the food; she kept her attention glued to the predator she'd seen stalking Derek moments before.

Eliza Crowe's sleek black hair was styled in a tight chignon, and her mask was wreathed in black feathers with sparkling rhinestones. The feathers climbed up in a tuft above her head, which made her easy to spot across the ballroom. She wore a sleeveless black gown with iridescent panels that reminded Lexi of the black crows she'd seen on the roadside. Lexi pressed her lips together and willed the ball of nerves between her shoulders to relax. Eliza would not win tonight.

The first bachelor stepped forward next to JoNelle, who opened the bidding at ten thousand dollars. Lexi's mouth dropped open when the man was awarded to the highest bidder a half a minute later at the sweet price of sixty-five thousand dollars. Lexi's palms were sweating in her purple gloves as she considered how much preparation Eliza must have put into her plan if she really thought she had a chance to win Derek.

Eliza walked toward the center of the room and then stopped to whisper to a couple dressed in elegant evening wear. The woman's teal gown reminded Lexi of a peacock, and the man held a mask that resembled a fox. They laughed and watched the stage. Eliza leaned toward the woman and whispered something else before walking to a table with two men. What if Eliza wasn't planning to purchase Derek after all? She could have teamed up with anyone in her quest to sabotage Derek. Lexi's mouth went dry. She'd arrived at this ball intending to watch and make sure that Eliza didn't win, but now she wasn't sure who her rival might be.

Lexi clenched her hands into fists as the next bachelor went for seventy-six thousand dollars. She scanned the crowd and made eye contact with Derek. With a squeak, she stepped to the side and ducked behind a professional basketball player. She gripped her bidding paddle and moved surreptitiously through the crowd along the back wall in semi-darkness. Derek was the twelfth bachelor up for auction, and Lexi didn't have much time left to figure out the best strategy to protect his photography business, keep Eliza's grabby hands off her man, and save their relationship.

Chapter 27

Derek kept catching sight of the woman in the purple ball gown, but it was only a glimpse before she disappeared again. Every time he saw her, he wanted to leap off the stage and remove her mask to see if jade eyes hid beneath the rim of rhinestones, feathers, and glitter.

JoNelle had instructed all the bachelors to appear confident and happy because they didn't have anything to worry about. Derek looked at the center of the room and his mouth tightened into a thin line. Eliza sat near two men who, by the looks of the expensive cut of their tuxedos, were probably sponsors. They sipped from wine glasses, and Eliza appeared cool and poised, her bidding paddle resting on the table in front of her. Her demeanor changed when the announcer started reading Derek's bio; she straightened, picked up her paddle, and smiled at Derek as if he were a plate of lobster. Derek forced himself to look away from Eliza and smile at the crowd. He prayed that someone, anyone, besides Eliza would win the bid.

JoNelle kept upping the starting bid as the night progressed, so Derek's spot opened up with a bid of fifty-five thousand dollars. The amount of money was dizzying when

Derek thought of all the ways he could use even half of that. But he stood up straighter and smiled wider, because the cause was a good one. The number of refugees tonight's benefit could help was just as staggering as the bidding prices—the goal of one million dollars didn't seem insurmountable anymore.

Someone in the crowd called out a bid for seventy thousand dollars. The woman wearing a teal gown was not Eliza, so Derek breathed a sigh of relief. But then Eliza stood and waved her paddle. "One hundred thousand dollars for Derek Mitchell," she called out, her face triumphant.

Several people stopped talking and turned to stare at Eliza. Derek narrowed his eyes, studying the two men next to her. Their eyes flicked to his and he straightened once again, smoothing his features.

"Wonderful!" JoNelle clapped. "We have a bid from Eliza Crowe for one hundred thousand dollars for Derek Mitchell." She paused and scanned the crowd, where several people clapped appreciatively toward Eliza as if she had won him already.

With a jolt, Derek realized that no one was bidding against her. His breath hitched as he watched JoNelle in slow motion, gavel in hand, step back to the stand where she would finalize the sale.

"One million dollars for bachelor number twelve," a clear voice shouted from the back of the ballroom.

The sea of glittering ball gowns and expensive tuxedos parted to reveal the woman in purple holding up her bidding paddle. The number was 117, printed in black on her white card. Derek shook his head as the rush of voices reached him.

"Did I hear that correctly?" JoNelle asked as she stepped forward.

The beautiful blonde with cascading purple, white, and gold flowers trailing from her mask held her paddle up higher. "Yes, one million dollars for Derek Mitchell!"

Applause erupted all over the room as the gavel fell. Derek stared at the woman, her stance, the way she held the paddle high above her head. It was all familiar, and his gut twisted as a dozen theories swirled in his head.

But none of those theories were as powerful as the words he heard next.

"And the highest bidder is number one-seventeen, Kauai's newest billionaire. She has worked for several years with Jordan Burke Enterprises, and recently the company exploded on the international market, making her worth just over a billion dollars. Congratulations to the beautiful and generous Lexi Burke."

Chapter 28

exi's face flamed underneath the mask, and her insides writhed in agony as she watched the shock slide over Derek's face. As the crowd moved to congratulate her, she lost sight of Derek and dropped her paddle to the ground. They weren't supposed to know it was her. She hadn't put her name on anything, but somehow they knew. She thought back to the check-in that night and the knowing look the man had given her when he'd handed her the bidding number—"Burke Enterprises, huh? Guess you're going to make a splash tonight."

Lexi had been speechless. The fact that he even knew about her business was confusing, but now it made sense. All of the applications had to be vouched for so that people could actually afford to pay cash for the bachelors they bid on. They had done their homework, but because it was a masquerade ball, she thought there might be anonymity involved in the actual bidding.

By the time Lexi made her way to the front of the room, the last bachelor had been sold for a healthy sum of one hundred twenty-five thousand dollars. She should've been smiling because she had just helped to change the world and Derek's life in the same night, but she kept seeing his face when they announced her name. The shock and betrayal cut to Lexi's core. On her way to the masquerade ball, she'd convinced herself that it wouldn't be so bad if Derek found out that she was rich, but JoNelle had announced that Lexi was Kauai's newest *billionaire*. Lexi would just have to explain to Derek that she really wasn't a billionaire. Burke Enterprises must have increased in value.

"Oh, there you are, Lexi dear." JoNelle came up beside her. "That was impressive. We'd like to get some pictures, if you don't mind. Your costume is absolutely divine, by the way."

She motioned for Lexi to follow her onto the stage, where a group of men in sport coats and tuxedos stood. The group shifted, and there was Derek in his striking gray sport coat and hair spiked in all the right places. His new camera sat next to him, the supple leather strap hanging off the table. He didn't look at Lexi.

"Okay, Derek, work your magic," JoNelle said.

He nodded and adjusted the camera over his neck. Then he climbed off the stage and focused on Lexi. She turned to JoNelle with a questioning look.

"Oh, Derek had a fantastic idea. He thought it would be great to have us take a picture of him taking a picture of you."

Lexi forced a smile. "Yes, that's nice." She saw another photographer to the side of Derek with his camera aimed on the two of them. Lexi tilted her head toward Derek, but she didn't smile. Her lips could be described as a demure pout, and if someone looked too close, they might see her bottom lip trembling slightly. She held the pose until the photographer grabbed the shots he wanted.

"Let's have a few of you together now," JoNelle said.

Derek climbed back on stage, leaving his camera hanging from his neck. He stood next to Lexi and when his fingers brushed hers, it was like a flash of heat.

"Derek, I couldn't let Eliza win that bid," Lexi whispered.

"Later." He smiled for the camera until JoNelle announced that they could leave.

Derek offered his arm to Lexi as they walked off the stage, but she could feel the anger radiating off him like the tiki torches outside the building. He moved stiffly, and with each step Lexi felt like she was walking toward a boiling volcano. They exited the ballroom and stood in a semi-darkened hallway that led to the kitchen.

"One million dollars?" Derek said as soon as the door clicked shut behind them.

"I didn't know how much they were willing to spend. I wanted to put a stop to it quickly." Lexi grabbed his arm. "Derek, I'm sorry, but Eliza had something planned and I didn't want to risk you getting hurt."

Derek shrugged his arm from under her. "You vouched for me?" Derek spat. "This camera? How much did you have to shell out to get that little deal done?"

Lexi stepped back. The venom in his voice burned through her. He wasn't listening and he'd already jumped to the topic of his new job. She'd been right to be worried. "I didn't pay anything—"

"Oh, that's right, I'm sure you didn't. But Burke Enterprises did." Derek raked his fingers through the spiked part of his hair. "A billionaire? You never gave me a clue. I thought you were like me!"

"I am like you." Lexi ripped her mask off. It tangled with her curls, and she winced. "I've worked hard my entire life for every dollar and it paid off. Why does that make me a bad person?"

"You lied to me."

"No, I never lied, but I couldn't tell you everything when you were so busy bagging on anyone you thought had ten dollars more than you."

He rocked back on his heels. "Is that how you see me? Poor little Derek who can't make it on his own?"

Lexi rubbed a hand across her forehead. "No, that's how you see yourself. You're always comparing yourself to someone you think has more than you when you have everything right here. You have the life people would pay millions for." Lexi blew out a breath. "You've always had everything, but you're too busy going to your own pity party to see it."

Derek shook his head. "I don't understand."

"I don't expect you to, but you should at least try. Derek, don't you know me? I am not my money."

"But a billion dollars?" He looked down at the camera hanging from his neck and scowled. If he tried to give the camera back, Lexi would snap.

She had to get him to understand. "Derek, listen. I didn't even know I was worth that much until they announced it tonight. Jordan told me he was going to sell some of our factories in China. He must have made quite the profit. And they could be combining my total worth with all of Burke enterprises, so maybe I'm not a billionaire after all."

"It doesn't matter." Derek clenched his fist. "You're just as bad as every rich snob who's kicked me along the way. Maybe worse—at least I knew who was kicking me then."

Lexi gasped and shook her head. "You don't mean that."

"Well, you can vouch for someone else, because I'm through with this charade." Derek turned and stomped down the hall.

His footsteps pounded out a cadence that matched the blood pumping through Lexi's temples. An instant headache seared behind her eyes, and she slumped back against the wall, covering her face. Derek was a volcano, spewing lava everywhere. Even if Lexi fled Kauai, she'd still be covered in ash, her skin burned and raw, just like her heart.

Derek slammed his car into gear, cursing at the rusty piece of junk as the engine sputtered and groaned to life. A new car to Lexi would be like pocket change. He punched the dash and cried out when a jolting pain shot through his wrist. He wanted to feel the pain—a physical pain instead of the emotional turmoil boiling his insides.

How could he be so stupid? He'd ignored all the signs: Lexi lived in Princeville, she'd quit her job, she didn't have another job, and she spent her days painting on the beach. Without closing his eyes, Derek could conjure her up like some ethereal ghost. A flash of her golden hair, her soft mouth with that curve in her upper lip, the way she kissed him until a fire roared inside strong enough it might never go out. All that was left now were the burning embers of betrayal.

Chapter 29

Somehow Lexi made it home and crawled into bed. She'd thought about calling Jordan to vent her sorrow, but she didn't dare. He would just insist that she come home to Chicago.

Sunday morning, she rose early and drove to Ke'e Beach. She wasn't looking for Derek. He wouldn't be there this early. She was looking for solitude.

Lexi started hiking the trail down from the beach. The tears made it hard for her to avoid the tree roots that wound surreptitiously across the path. She stumbled and fell hard when she reached Hanakapi'ai Beach.

The burn on her knees and scuffed hands broke the remaining timbers in her dam; Lexi sat down right there and sobbed. She rubbed her eyes, wondering why the people she loved the most were taken from her. She loved Derek, and she thought her love would be enough for him to overcome his disdain for excessive wealth, but it wasn't. She took a shaky breath and admitted to herself that this was different from her parents' death. It was her fault for keeping the truth from Derek. She'd convinced herself that it was the only way, but seeing Derek's face last night—the look of betrayal etched into his features—was proof that she'd been wrong.

Something furry rubbed along her calves. Lexi started and looked down to see Mango winding around her legs, his bushy tail flicking her ankles. "Oh, it's you. Aloha, kitty."

Lexi ran her hand along Mango's back, and then impulsively picked the cat up and held him close. Mango purred and rubbed her neck with his head. "What am I going to do?" Lexi whispered. Her heart felt like one of Pika's coconuts that had cracked open, and Derek was the one holding the machete.

A vision of the Na Pali coastline came to her mind. She remembered telling Derek that she couldn't think of anything that would make her ever want to leave this place, but she would have to amend that statement because she'd never considered the pain of a broken heart. Kauai wasn't a paradise without Derek.

Thinking of her broken heart led to thoughts of Shawn. He'd declared his love for her, but settled for just friends. Maybe he was right when he warned her that people with money have to live a different life even if they don't want to. Shawn was a good man. He probably had a more accurate idea of Lexi's worth than she did, but he'd never acted like he was interested in her for her money.

She wasn't desperate for a relationship, but she *was* desperate to fix things with Derek. She clutched her phone. She dialed Gracie and Jordan, but neither answered. Where was the advice hotline for billionaires when she needed it?

She found Shawn's picture in her contacts and stared at his face. He spent more money on the highlights in his hair than Derek probably did for his entire wardrobe. She pushed call.

"I don't know what to do." Her words tumbled over each other as she confided her deceit and greatest fears to Shawn.

"Do you love him?"

Lexi wiped the tears from her cheek. "Yes."

"Then you have to find him and tell him. If he can't see that you're authentic, then he doesn't deserve you."

Lexi's heart fractured in another jagged line with Shawn's words. "I don't know if he'll listen."

"On his own, away from the crowds. Maybe things will be different."

"It might be too late."

"If it is, then I'm here, Lex," Shawn said. "Second best is better than nothing at all."

"Oh, Shawn. I'm sorry. I don't want to hurt you."

"It hurts me to hear the tears in your voice. It hurts me when you're unhappy. I still love you, Lexi. So go find this guy before I do. I'll be waiting, and I might be praying that a large fish swallows him."

Lexi chuckled. "I'll try. But you deserve someone better than me—someone who can love you with their whole heart."

"I'm a patient man," Shawn said. "Good luck."

Lexi ended the call and hugged the phone to her chest. The pain in her heart was more excruciating than any emotional pain she'd felt before. Her heart *hurt*, with a physical hurt that left her gasping for breath. She looked up at the skyline filled with the brooding mountains of the Na Pali coast, and she knew where she'd find Derek.

Her legs were shaky when she stood, but a surge of energy pushed her forward, and soon she was running up the trail and skidding past sharp rocks and branches toward Ke'e Beach.

When she got there, she sprinted to her Jeep and drove the long, winding road around the island toward Waimea Canyon.

She passed the overlook where Derek had taken photographs of her before he'd lost his camera, before he'd been put up for auction. The clouds grew darker and heavier the farther she drove.

Her Jeep groaned as the incline rose, and she pressed the gas pedal down. The sign for the Pu'u o Kila Lookout came into view, and Lexi wrenched the steering wheel to the right, skidding to a stop in the empty parking lot. Empty except for a certain rust-colored Subaru driven by the man she loved.

A fine mist hung heavy in the air. She put on a rain jacket, her heart tightening with fear and laced with hope. If she could just tell Derek that he meant more to her than anything else in the world. His love for the island made her feel at home, and she never wanted to leave. If he would listen for one minute, then maybe he could forgive her deceit.

Lexi hopped out of the Jeep and scanned the area for Derek; then she hurried up the trailhead, stopping at the overlook that had taken her breath away the first time she'd seen it. She sent up a silent prayer for help to find Derek and that his heart might be softened before she caught up with him.

A quiet peace filled her as she looked at the canvas in the Creator's hand with colors she'd never imagined before. Greens with a vibrant golden lining and blues muted by the gray skies above. The panorama before her spoke to her soul, filling her senses with a reverence for the gifts that God had given her on this island—a chance to find herself and to learn what was most important.

Lexi's throat clenched and her eyes filled with tears. Derek was the most important thing to her in that moment. She turned from the vista and walked forward along the red trail, searching for him.

The mist turned to rain that fell softly at first, and then harder. Red mud squelched around Lexi's tennis shoes. She reached a point in the trail where it curved around large boulders and traveled down a steep hill. Water trickled along the rocks, and Lexi looked up at the sky, wondering how long the rain would last. She recalled the waterfalls from Derek's photography and how he'd explained that they sprouted with every rainstorm.

She put one foot in front of the other, holding on to the rocks as she climbed down the slope. The rock she'd just placed her foot against rolled. It happened faster than the rain falling from the sky, yet Lexi saw it in slow motion: the trail collapsed and muddy water rained down on her as she fell. She slammed into a boulder and cried out, the air pushed from her lungs with such force that she was left with searing pain, gasping for air. She moaned and heaved, trying to stop her lungs from convulsing. When she finally sucked in a breath, her head tingled. She lifted her fingertips to her scalp and recognized the warm thickness of blood.

Lexi kept still, breathing slowly, trying to decide what to do next. Her foot was cold, and when she wiggled her toes she realized that her leg was hanging halfway off a rock ledge. With one hand, she felt for the edge of the drop-off, gripping the rock. The rock sat like a pedestal in the ravine with one side against the muddy mountainside, and Lexi was in the center of it. The cliff rose up sharply away from the trail, and the boulder was just far enough from the outer rim she'd been standing on that it would take a giant leap to reach safety. She closed her eyes and prayed for help to the God who had created the incredible vista, the raindrops, the red mud, and Derek.

Chapter 30

The rain pelted Derek's face, but he lifted his chin, letting the warm moisture roll down his cheeks and drip from his beard. It was past time to turn back, and he'd gone farther than safety recommended in this storm. He'd replayed his conversation with Lexi last night—every angry word. It contrasted painfully with every encounter he'd had with her before last night. The Lexi he knew in his heart was not the shadow her money created in his mind. The peace of the Na Pali coastline had given him a chance to open his eyes and see that his judgment against Lexi and anyone with wealth was wrong. He'd let his own insecurities blind him to the beautiful gifts God had given him on the island—not only in the raw nature surrounding him, but in Lexi. He clenched his jaw until it trembled. What if it was too late to fix things?

He scraped his boots on the rocks and flipped his hood up. This part of the trail was always tricky, and for a moment he considered waiting until the rain stopped, but then he heard a cry. It was too loud to be a bird, and birds were silent in the rain. It had to be human, and strangely, he thought it might be

Lexi. His heart ricocheted in his chest, and panic flared through his veins.

He paused, looking around, listening to the rush of rain mimicking the sounds of the ocean below. It couldn't have been Lexi, but her voice reverberated in his head. Lexi was everywhere around him. He could imagine her smelling the flowers and hiking the trail with determination and a smile. Of course he would think of her when he heard that noise. He'd made his decision: pride was a lonely partner, and he didn't intend to live his life in agony. Lexi was waiting for him somewhere. He just had to find her and ask for her forgiveness.

He grabbed onto a tree branch and pulled himself farther along. Stumbling on rocks, Derek noticed that a mini-slide had occurred higher up the trail. The large boulder that marked the upper ledge streamed dark red with mud.

But wait, that wasn't just dirt . . . Derek lurched forward, scrambling up the trail. A line of blood shimmered along the indentations of the boulder, and Derek knew in his gut that it was Lexi's.

The mud ran thick around the rocks, and Derek had to go off-trail and climb through bushes and around trees to get to the top. He spied a neon-green running shoe caught against a jagged boulder. "Lexi! Lexi! I'm here!"

A moan answered his cries, and he looked to his right to find her curled on a rock, a hand to her head. He searched frantically until he saw a bush that he could grab. He held tight to the coarse bark and dropped down to the ledge, where Lexi lay dangerously close to the edge. "Don't move. I'm here. Can you hear me?"

She opened her eyes, the jade hue in crystal-clear focus, piercing Derek's soul. "You came," she whispered.

"Lexi, I'm an idiot. I'm so sorry. Please be okay. I'm here now. Can you move? Is your back okay?" His words came faster than the raindrops pelting his face.

"It's just my head. It hurts." Lexi reached her other hand up and touched the scruff on his cheek. "I love you."

Derek grasped her hand, his throat thick with emotion. She loved him, after he'd rejected her, humiliated her—after all he'd done to her. "I love you, too, Lexi Burke—my golden girl."

He was able to get her to her feet and pull her up the muddy surface, flinching every time she winced in pain. Once they reached even ground, he scooped her into his arms and hurried to his car. "I have a first aid kit. Let's take a look at your head."

She had a two-inch gash on the back of her head and was sucking in air like every breath hurt. Derek helped her apply pressure and settled her in the front seat of his car, with the seat reclined. He drove as quickly as he dared on the slick roads with his precious cargo. Minutes ticked by, and Lexi's breathing evened out. Derek spoke in hushed tones, keeping her alert. "You'll be okay. Head wounds bleed a lot, but it looked clean. How do you feel?"

"Glad that you found me," Lexi said.

"But you found me," Derek said. He glanced at her with a smile. "You're some kind of angel, aren't you?"

"Angels don't lie. Derek, I'm so sorry that I wasn't honest with you."

Derek held up his hand. "No, I'm sorry. If I hadn't acted the way I did, you wouldn't have been afraid to tell me that you're, you know, a billionaire."

Lexi laughed weakly. "I promise that I didn't know about being a billionaire. That was news to me, and I still haven't confirmed it."

"I'm not angry anymore, Lexi. I've been up here all morning asking God to help me fix things. I was completely unfair to you. You didn't need to tell me your personal financial situation, and if I'm being the kind of man that I should be, your money shouldn't matter."

Lexi sighed. "Thank you. I'm sorry that I was living a Hawaiian masquerade this whole time. From now on, my mask is off."

The relief in her voice pricked Derek's soul, and he vowed to earn her trust, respect, and love. She was a finder of lost souls. Derek could see each moment he'd known her, from the first day when she held the little girl in the store, to spending time with her friend who was struggling, to the intense scene last night when she'd stepped out from the crowd like a vision and rescued him. "Thank you. I need to tell you that GlobePhoto contacted me last night. They were confused about some kind of arrangement that Eliza was trying to make between us, using some of my photos and hers combined in a tourist package deal. It was all Eliza. I don't understand why she was trying to exploit me when she has plenty of talent herself, but you, you . . . saved me..."

"It only cost a million dollars." Lexi chuckled, and the sound warmed Derek's heart.

He helped Lexi into the hospital. While she waited to be checked out, she held his hand. "I would've given a lot more than a million dollars for you, Derek."

Derek leaned forward and kissed her gently. "I know. I didn't understand how that much money could ever be a good thing, but I do now. Money is a tool, like a machete. With the right intent, it can support a family, help a friend, or even fix a water heater. Your soul is beautiful, Lexi."

Lexi kissed him until the nurse returned to stitch up her head.

Chapter 31

exi smiled when Derek parked near Ke'e Beach the following week. Her head had healed nicely, and she'd had plenty of time to recover while Derek worked overtime to design a new logo and build up a portfolio for his new job. There was a light in his eyes that made Lexi grin every time she saw him.

"So, we're back to where it all began?" Lexi asked as she trudged through the sand with Derek carrying the snorkeling gear and his new camera.

"I thought if we looked hard enough, we might see those kissing sea turtles again." Derek checked the case on his waterproof camera and double-checked the strap before sliding it over his neck.

Lexi laughed. "Any bets this time regarding those turtles?"

"Hmm—if we see them, then you have to let me teach you how to chop coconuts."

She moved his camera out of the way and placed a hand on his chest. "And if we don't, then you promise to keep searching with me until we find them."

Derek arched an eyebrow. "That could take a long time."

Lexi nodded, and then she lifted up on her toes to kiss him. She put her arms around his neck and whispered in his ear. "Maybe forever."

"I certainly hope so," he replied, before kissing her until everything else melted away but the paradise between them.

The End

Please enjoy this sneak peek of Jordan's story…#2 Burke Billionaire Romance

The Billionaire's Stray Heart

CHAPTER ONE

Jordan Burke checked his watch as he walked from his office in downtown Chicago to the lunch meeting that would start in ten minutes. The billionaire owner of Burke Enterprises could have taken the company limo, but walking was faster in the midday traffic and it was a good excuse for him to get some exercise.

He quickened his pace only to be held up by a red hand signal at the stop light. He tapped his foot impatiently as he waited for the light to change.

"Jordy! Jordy, wait up!"

Jordan straightened and then turned at the sound of the nickname that his sister, Lexi, still called him. A woman with dark hair pulled back in a ponytail tugged on the leash of two dogs that were fast approaching him. The border collie stayed alert at her side, but the larger golden doodle tugged on the leash, following his nose toward Jordan.

"Jordy. Heel." The dog hesitated, glanced at the woman, and then nosed against Jordan's hand.

"I'm sorry. This one's in training." She tugged on the leash again.

Jordan laughed. "His name is Jordy?"

The woman tilted her head and gave a hesitant smile. "Yes."

Jordan pointed at himself. "That's my nickname, but only my sister calls me that."

She laughed and Jordan noticed the musical sound—bright and beautiful, just like the light in her hazel eyes. "Well, don't feel bad. I've met lots of dogs named Maddie, which is my nickname. My friend told me I should take it as a compliment that my name is so popular for dogs."

Jordan laughed again and felt some of the tightness in his shoulders ease up. He patted Jordy's head, noting that his namesake had a curly golden coat that was well-groomed.

"This dog sure is a beauty."

She nodded. "He is that. His owners were considering giving him up because he was so hyper." She smiled down at the dog. "But you're doing better now, aren't you Jordy?" She looked up at Jordan and her cheeks pinked. "I'm a dog trainer, so both of these guys are my clients."

Jordan's heart did something funny when he noticed her cheeks flush. It almost felt like it'd skipped a beat. He took a step closer to Maddie. She had a dimple in her left cheek and a small nose with a light smattering of freckles. "You must be good at your job then. Lucky guy." He rubbed behind the dog's ears forcing himself to look away from the sparkle in Maddie's eyes.

"Thank you." The border collie shifted his weight back and forth and looked up at Maddie.

The street signal began chirping, and Jordan looked up to see the walk signal. "Well, good luck with those two." He lifted his hand in a wave and hurried across the street. Once his feet hit the sidewalk again, he hesitated, looking back once. Maddie had turned toward the park and for a moment Jordan wished he'd asked her for her phone number. He shrugged. Who was he kidding? The only dates he went on were those arranged through his secretary. He glanced at his watch again and frowned. The old Jordy might not have worried about being late to a lunch meeting if it meant getting the number of a pretty girl, but that guy had been replaced by the new and improved version. Jordan Burke was a man of business.

CHAPTER TWO

Seven months. That's how long it had been since Jordan Burke's last date. His younger sister, Lexi, had done her best to remind him of that fact and persuade him to go on a date tonight. Jordan stood in the waiting area of the fancy Thai restaurant waiting for his date to show up.

His date was Lexi's best friend, Gracie Cardulo. Jordan hadn't seen her for at least three years, but he still remembered how beautiful she was with her lithe dancer's body, olive skin and dark hair. He wondered if Lexi had twisted her friend's arm to schedule this date as well.

Jordan didn't really look at it as an actual date, but the thought made him wonder, if he had time to date, who would he go out with? His heart did that funny skip-beat thing again when the woman walking those dogs came to his mind. Maddie. It had only been a few hours ago and he mentally kicked himself for not getting her number.

"Well, you're actually here." Gracie sidled up next to Jordan, her face lifting in a familiar smile. Jordan snapped back to attention and smiled as he looked down at Gracie. "I'm here. But don't look so surprised. How are you?" He gave her a hug. They had texted back and forth in preparation for the date so Jordan knew that she'd come to Chicago to audition for a part in a ballet studio.

Gracie smiled. "Well, the auditions are over but I won't know for a couple more days whether I got the part or not."

Jordan's phone buzzed in his pocket and he reached to grab it, but paused when he realized that Gracie was waiting for him to reply. He cleared his throat. "Oh, well, I'm sure you'll get the part and if you don't, it's their loss."

Gracie put her hand on his arm. "Thanks for that. I really don't know what's going to happen with my career. I'm probably too old to try out for the part that I did."

Jordan raised his eyebrows. "Aren't you the same age as Lexi? Thirty-two, thirty-three? If you're old what does that make me?"

Gracie laughed. "I'm only twenty-eight, but when it comes to ballet, old was a few years back. I'm really pushing it now. But don't worry, you have a lot of good years left in you." She winked.

Jordan's phone buzzed again and his lips twitched. "Do you mind if I get this real quick?"

Gracie lifted one shoulder and let it drop. "Go ahead."

Jordan looked at his screen and saw that the call wasn't coming in from China so he could ignore it for now. He swiped down sending an automatic text message and slipped the phone back into his pocket. "Sorry about that."

Before Gracie could answer, the maître d' arrived and led them through the dining area to a cozy table for two infused with ambient light. They had a few minutes to talk over the menu and place their order before Jordan's cell phone pinged with incoming texts. He shook his head, holding up the phone. "Work never stops." He hurriedly answered the texts and then slid the phone into his pocket. "So how do you like Chicago?"

"It's a beautiful city—so much history," Gracie answered. "I love that the arts play such a role here. Please tell me that you've taken time to appreciate some of that."

"I always meant to double with Lexi and her dates to some of the concerts and such, but then, she never dated much when she was here either." Jordan struggled to think of the last thing he'd done for fun that was unique to the city. "I can see the St. Patrick's Day parade from my office window."

Gracie leaned forward. "But I have a feeling you didn't see much of it this year."

"They dye the river green." Jordan tried to remember if he had even looked out his window this past March. He shrugged. "I guess I need to get out more."

"You said it, not me," Gracie replied. The answer indicated that his sister had filled her in on the sad state of Jordan's social life.

A few minutes later, their meals arrived and Jordan made an effort to ask Gracie specific questions that would take the focus off him. She explained the role she'd auditioned for in the well-known Swan Lake ballet. Jordan was about to ask her what her favorite part was when his phone started ringing again. He gave Gracie an apologetic look before pulling it out of his jacket pocket. "I have to take this—it's China. If you'll excuse me for a moment." Without waiting for Gracie to answer, Jordan stood and walked toward the back of the restaurant. He answered the call—another urgent matter concerning the new manufacturing plant in China that created molds for plastics.

When he ended the call he was surprised to see that it had taken him eight minutes to sort out the problem. He approached the table, trying to assess Gracie's mood before he sat down. She was toying with her salad, her brow furrowed as she gazed at the other diners.

"I'm really sorry about that."

"Don't you have a secretary or an assistant for phone calls?" Gracie asked.

Jordan nodded. "I do, but these are calls that have been transferred to me. Lately I'm fielding a lot more calls than I used to."

Gracie leaned forward. "That sounds like your assistant isn't doing their job. You need to hire more people, Jordan. You should be able to go out to dinner without fielding calls from China."

Jordan looked down at the fish on his plate, now growing cold. What she'd said was true, but he'd also started his company from scratch, running everything himself, staying up late every night trying to coordinate things with the difference in time zones from Chicago to China. "I probably do need to hire more help. It's pretty tricky finding someone with the right skill set, and especially someone who can speak Mandarin Chinese."

Gracie pursed her lips. "If you really wanted to, you could hire enough people that you would never have to answer another phone call from China. Or do you like having your phone be the boss of you?"

Jordan bristled. Gracie's words hit the target that others had painted on his chest—that he was a control freak, a micro-manager. He took a breath and blew it out. "Let's not talk about my job, that's boring." He straightened his tie. "So you said you're not certain what you're going to do next. If things don't pan out with this audition, where will you go?"

Gracie hesitated, as if trying to decide to let him change the subject. She set down her fork. "Lexi really wants me to come back to Kauai and work with her for Burke's Higher Steps. I'm just not sure I'm ready to retire from dancing yet."

Jordan opened his mouth to reply but was interrupted by the ringing of his phone. He groaned and looked at Gracie. She arched one eyebrow, cocking her head, almost daring him to answer it. He looked at the screen and recognized his main liaison to China. "I have to answer this. This is my second in command over in China. He never calls unless it's an emergency. He shoveled in a large bite of fish and mumbled. "Could you order us some dessert?" He hesitated with his finger over the screen waiting for Gracie to reply.

She sighed. "Go ahead. I'll order dessert."

Ten minutes later, Jordan gulped for air. He'd spoken as quickly as he could, people staring at him, possibly wondering how a blond haired guy in Illinois could speak Chinese. He sat at the table and his phone chimed with several incoming texts. He quickly scrolled through them, forwarding some for his assistant and answering others. He heard the clink of silverware and saw that Gracie had pushed aside her plate.

"Is dessert coming?"

Gracie licked her lips. She wasn't smiling. "I didn't order dessert. I think I'm just going to go. I can tell it's a really busy night for you."

Jordan panicked. If Lexi heard how he had treated her best friend…he groaned inwardly. He was in trouble no matter what he did now. "No, wait. I'm sorry. I'm just—I don't know what to do."

Gracie gave him a sympathetic look. "You know the saddest thing?"

Jordan straightened. "No. What?"

"You're a billionaire and yet you're working probably as many hours as you did when you started this business with nothing."

Her words poured down on him like acid rain. "Look, I'm sorry. I told Lexi I'm not in a place where I can date right now. You're a beautiful woman and I'm sure you're fun to be around, but I just don't have time to date right now. I hope we can still be friends."

Gracie stood and straightened her dress. "Friends? I don't think you're ready for friends either. Maybe you should start with a dog." She adjusted the strap on her purse and gave him a flat smile. "Thanks for dinner. I hope you have a good night."

Gracie took a step forward and Jordan's phone rang again. She glanced back as if giving him one last chance, but Jordan could recognize by the distinct ring tone that this call was more important than any other he'd answered that night. He lifted his fingers in a wave and put the phone to his ear answering in Chinese as Gracie walked out of the restaurant.

By the time Jordan paid the bill, ate another bite of curry and exited the restaurant, he had answered three more calls. He was angry with himself and also with Gracie's impatience. She hadn't seemed to understand that he really was the owner of a billion-dollar company.

Jordan was deep in thought as he walked down the street to where he had parked his car. He cut through an alleyway and walked about ten steps before he realized he'd made a wrong turn. He pivoted but his heart slammed into his chest when four young men stepped out in front of him.

"Okay, pretty boy, you know the drill. Hand over your cash." The hooded figure to his right spoke in clear English so Jordan couldn't pretend that he didn't understand.

Jordan hesitated, they weren't that far from the street entrance, but he didn't want to take his eyes off of the four gang members in front of him in case one of them made a sudden move. He swallowed, trying to come up with a response to keep things cool, but adrenaline pumped through his veins when he saw the glint of steel as one of them flicked a knife back and forth. He could easily throw his wallet out for them, but something told him that when they saw the seven-hundred dollars in bills inside that he wouldn't leave this mugging unscathed.

The alleyway was too dark. He couldn't tell if they had guns or not. Briefly he wondered if it was worth the risk to run to the other end of the alley. And then he thought of an idea. He began speaking rapidly in Chinese, putting his hand up and gesturing back and forth. When he paused to catch his breath, one of the young men took a step forward and held up the knife.

"Mister, we know you speak English. We heard you talking on the phone. Hand over your wallet and we'll let you go." The young man took a step forward and Jordan took a step back. He stepped on something soft, yet firm, and he heard a yelp, followed by a loud bark. Jordan stumbled into a pile of boxes, sending them toppling to the ground. They crashed across the alleyway and a vicious barking started up, different than the yelping at his feet. Jordan backed against the wall with the gang members shouting, demanding his wallet. His pulse drummed so hard he could hear it accompanying the sounds around him. The barking intensified as two large dogs streaked past him, ramming right into the gang members. Two of them fell to the ground and Jordan took advantage of the distraction, sprinting toward the end of the alley. With his breaths coming fast, he gasped when he saw the brick wall in front of him. A dead end.

Learn more about The Billionaire's Stray Heart and other romance novels at www.rachellechristensen.com

Acknowledgements

I'd like to thank Gelato Publishing for the opportunity to write in the Destination Billionaire Series. This has been so much fun and I'm thrilled about the possibilities for the Burke Billionaire Romance Line. The only way it could be better is if I could head to Kauai again for more research.

Thank you to Christina Dymock for your excellent advice, wordsmithing tools, and friendship. Thanks to my early readers: Patrick and Necia Jolley, Lucy McConnell, Gracie Christensen, Cathy Jeppsen, Cami Checketts, and Lisa Whitesides. I appreciate your feedback and enthusiasm for the characters in this book.

A huge thanks to my family for supporting my crazy writing habit. My husband, Steve, and my kids all helped brainstorm different points in this novel, and they cheered me on when I reported my daily word count.

And to you, Reader, thank you for taking the time to read my book. Without you, none of this work would matter. I am truly grateful for each of my readers, for the kind words and encouragement you share, and for your kindred spirits found among pages and pages of words.

I'm especially grateful to God for creating this beautiful world and blessing me with talents and experiences to open my eyes to infinite possibilities.

Photo by Erin Summerill

About the Author

Rachelle is a mother of five who writes mystery/suspense, nonfiction, and women's fiction. She solves the case of the missing shoe on a daily basis. She enjoys raising chickens and laughing with her husband. She graduated cum laude from Utah State University with a degree in psychology and a minor in music.

Rachelle is the award-winning author of twenty books, including *The Soldier's Bride (a Kindle Scout Selection)*, *Diamond Rings Are Deadly Things*, *Hawaiian Masquerade*, and *Christmas Kisses: An Echo Ridge Anthology*. Her novella, "Silver Cascade Secrets," was included in the Rone Award–winning *Timeless Romance Anthology, Fall Collection*.

Join Rachelle's VIP mailing list to learn more about upcoming books and get your free book at www.rachellechristensen.com.

Your Free Book is Waiting

FROM AWARD-WINNING
AND BESTSELLING AUTHOR
Rachelle J. Christensen

Take one park in autumn, mix in a handsome stranger, a daring heroine, murder, chocolate peanut butter brownies, mystery, and a few kisses and you'll see why *Silver Cascade Secrets* has everything you need to satisfy your cravingsfor a good read.

amazon kindle **nook** **kobo** iBooks

★ ★ ★ ★ ★

Visit www.rachellechristensen.com